P A L M

SPRINGS

BABYLON

Sizzling Stories from the
Desert Playground of the Stars

P A L M
S P R I N G S
B A B Y L O N

R A Y   M U N G O

St. Martin's Press   New York

◄ Her royal highness Barbara Sinatra steps out in Palm Springs in style. (Photo courtesy Paul Pospesil Collection)

Graphics courtesy Palm Springs Chamber of Commerce

ISBN   0-312-06438-1 (paperback)

Design by Maura Fadden Rosenthal

10   9   8

Contents

Preface   1

A Social History of Palm Springs   8

In the Beginning   36

Charlie Farrell
Some Kind of Racquet   44

Culver Nichols, Pioneer   53

Who's Got It?
The Wealthiest People in Palm Springs   56

The Mob and the Dunes:
Wide Open Spaces in Little Vegas   60

Ric-Su-Dar
The Zanucks in Palm Springs   68

Going His Way
Der Bingle in the Desert   74

Desert Desilu Follies   80

Hope Springs Infernal
The Man and His Mountains   86

Ring-a-Ding-Ding
Hooray for the King   94

Do You Know the Way to Danny Kaye?
Palm Springs Streets Named After Celebrities   112

Normandy Remembered:
Is Errol Flynn Turning Over in His Grave?   114

What Will the Old Ladies Think?
Liberace in Palm Springs   118

Sally's Balls   128

Blue Suede Shoes
Elvis Alone   132

Bono Knows:
Some Vital Statistics about Palm Springs   136

Piece of the Rock
Hudson in the Desert with Tom and Marc   140

The Hidden Power
Walter Annenberg as Emperor of the Desert   144

Royalty of Piety
Jim and Tammy Faye Sleaze It Up in P.S.   154

Father of the Groom
Kirk Douglas in Palm Springs   157

Sonny Side of the Street
Former Cher Bimbo Goes His Own Way   160

Getting a Break Today   168

None But the Brave
U.S. Presidents in Palm Springs   170

Betty Bloomer Ford
Little Lady Takes on the Big Boys   178

Indian Givers
A Sioux A Sioux   183

Just Hangin' Around
The Divine One in the Desert   188

What's In a Name?
A Palm Springs Hoax   190

Back in the Saddle
Out Where a Friend Is a Friend   192

Quotes from the Notables
What They've Said About Palm Springs   198

A Little Champagne Music
Ah Vun, Ah Two   202

How Does She Look So Young?
Dinah Denies It   204

God's Waiting Room
The Gay Nineties   206

Palm Springs Phoenix   213

Preface

2

THIS BOOK IS in the spirit and likeness of its great predecessor, *Hollywood Babylon*, and Palm Springs, with its vast reputation as playground of the rich and famous, rivals any town for sheer decadence and excess. But Palm Springs Babylon is not the same culture as the Hollywood variety. The place has its own brand of social futility, scandal, drugs and death. Palm Springs is where the celebrities come to hide, after all—to party in seclusion behind security-gate walls. But the stories of what really goes on get around, and the sordid details of the occasional divorce or AIDS death leak into the papers.

Palm Springs is horrified. Palm Springs is amused. Palm Springs goes on, searching for new depths.

For purposes of this book, "Palm Springs" is not limited to the city itself, but includes surrounding ritzomaniac communities like Rancho Mirage (where Lucille Ball and Desi Arnaz built their weekend getaway villa accommodating seventy-five couples), Palm Desert (site of the world's largest man-made lake), Indian Wells (where the Grand Champions Resort just filed for Chapter 11), and La Quinta (the only town built around a luxury hotel).

◄ Starlets in the hot mineral baths at the Spa Hotel, site of the original Palm Springs. "One of these gals fainted and I had to give her mouth to mouth resuscitation," said photographer Frank Bogert. (Photo courtesy Frank Bogert Collection)

▲ Old and new Palm Springs mayors, Frank Bogert (L) and Sonny Bono, at the dedication of a statue of Bogert on horseback in front of City Hall, 1991. Bogert called Bono "chicken shit." (Photo courtesy Paul Pospesil Collection)

▶ Sultry Rita Hayworth, born Margarita Carmen Lansing in 1918, was a regular at the Racquet Club. (Photo courtesy Star File)

THIS BOOK ALSO profiles an attitude, a social history, of a unique and morally bankrupt community, a town devoted solely to the pursuit of pleasure. Palm Springs' history, which I have been researching as a special projects editor at *Palm Springs Life* magazine, is made up of hotels, nightclubs, bars, resorts, famous parties, cheats, real estate scams, bankruptcies, organized crime, fraudulent titles (the town founders, called "Judge" McCallum and "Doctor" Murray, were neither), Indian ripoffs, and private retreats (Annenberg, lately) so luxurious that heads of state gather there rather than in common imperial palaces.

There has always been an air of illusion about the place. Palm Springs is a mirage. The city fathers have long made a practice of exaggerating the local prosperity and even the weather reports to make Palm Springs look more attractive. This kind of fantasizing is still going on in the person of the mayor, Sonny Bono, who is very accessible and entertaining. He turned a burnout career as the former Mr. Cher into vast new celebrity, but he's fantasizing again when he says the 1990 Palm Springs Film Festival was "successful."

In January, 1991, Bono asked the City Council to forgive overdue loans of $50,000 to the Festival.

The desert offered the stars a place to let their hair down, to live it up, without the glare of publicity. When Kenneth Anger was writing *Hollywood Babylon,* he had the advantage of a huge body of published gossip of the most lurid sort, as the press had always been obsessed with Hollywood and its people. In Palm Springs, the really juicy stuff was covered up, suppressed. Still, in its own fashion Palm Springs was and is as rich in celebrity gossip and tales of the relentlessly powerful as anyplace on earth. Having pored through hundreds of archives, thousands of articles and dozens of books on the subject, I can say with conviction that nobody has even come close to telling the real story of Palm Springs—what went down back then, what's going down now in this amazing, spoiled little outpost.

▶ When blond Troy Donahue got ripped by the pool (and by Connie Stevens) in the film, *Palm Springs Weekend,* Spring Break was born. The picture was shot at what is now the Desert Palms Inn, largest gay- and lesbian-oriented resort in town. (Photo: Warner Bros. publicity still)

SAN BERNARDINO
MONA
ONTARIO
REDLAND
RIVERSIDE
CORONA
MT.
PERRIS
ELSINORE
HEMET
CAHUILLA
SAN JUAN CAPISTRANO
FALLBROOK
OCEANSIDE
ESCONDIDO
LA JOLLA

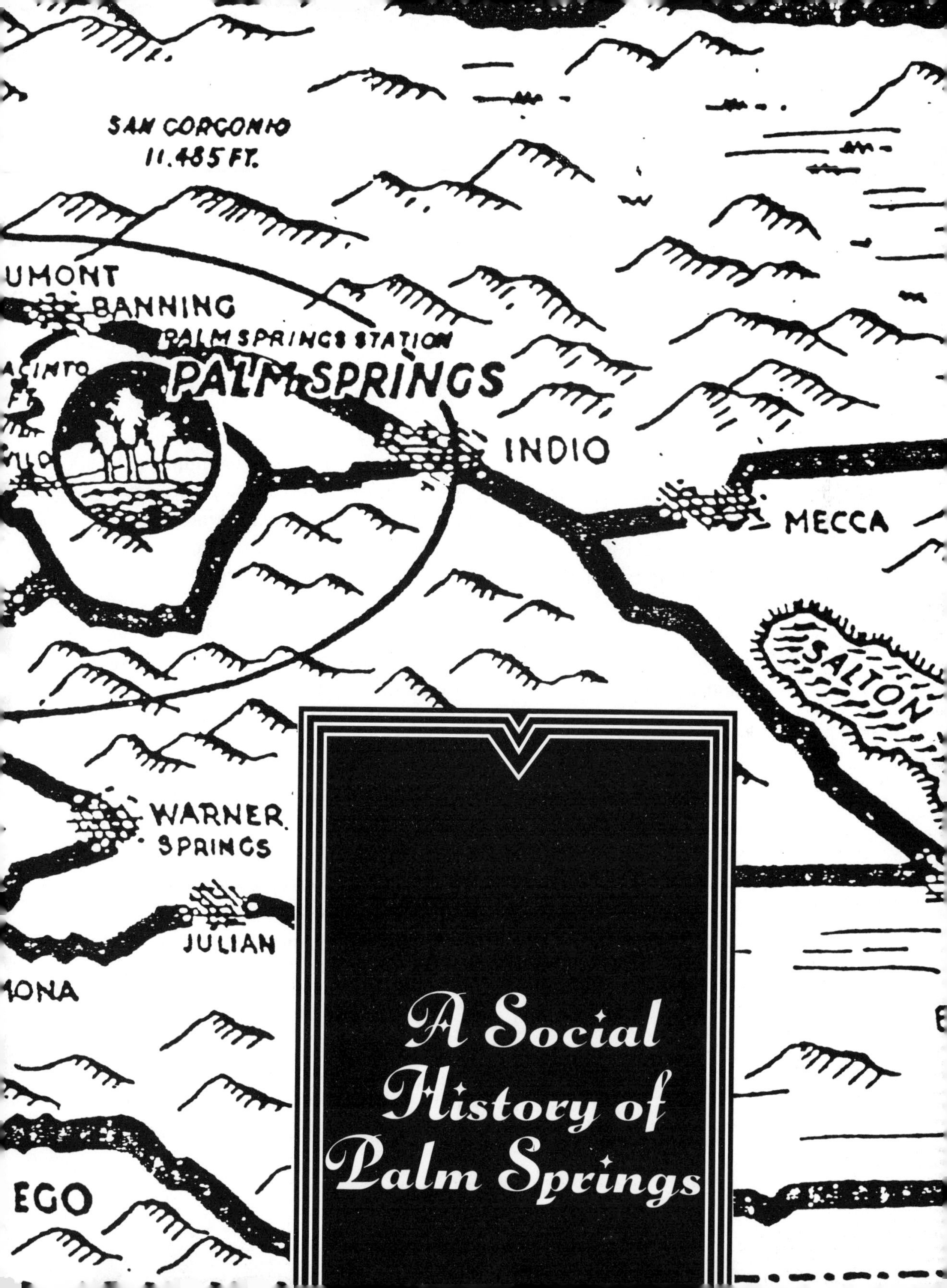

SAN GORGONIO
11,485 FT.

UMONT

BANNING

PALM SPRINGS STATION

PALM SPRINGS

ACINTO

INDIO

MECCA

SALTON

WARNER
SPRINGS

JULIAN

ONA

EGO

A Social
History of
Palm Springs

PALM SPRINGS! THE VERY name suggests California sunshine, palm trees, blue skies, hot water, health, shimmering desert mountains, Hollywood celebrities frolicking in swimming pools or on tennis courts, U.S. presidents and heads of state playing golf even in the kindly warmth of February, wealth and luxury beyond your wildest dreams.

Palm Springs the hidden, Palm Springs the demure, provides security and a veil for the misdeeds and private fantasies of the famous and rich. In Palm Springs they can party all weekend, let their hair down, drink into oblivion, easily obtain all drugs, keep their mistresses and boyfriends, go gay or bi- or pansexual, hide from the law or the press, feast on incomparable delicacies and enjoy priceless art treasures, and have it all without the glare of publicity, without the risk of exposure.

Until now. Your intrepid reporter, transported to a new life in the playground of southern California and assigned by *Palm Springs Life* magazine to write a business history of the town in conjunction with the 50th anniversary of the Chamber of Commerce, found chinks in the armor, startling revelations in the indiscretions of midnight champagne parties, wicked little stories that invariably began, "Don't print this in *Palm Springs Life*," and ended, "They managed to cover it up."

Like the time **Frank Sinatra** tossed **Ava Gardner** and **Lana Turner** out of his Tamarisk Country Club home in the middle of the night. Or when **Liberace** imported two French teenaged boys to share his vast collection of pornographic videos. Or the time **Frederick Loewe** passed his friend **Allan Keller** off as "Anna Maria von Steiner, world famous concert pianist and inspiration of *My Fair*

10

▲ "The village" seen in an aerial photo in the 1930s heyday of the stars. (Photo courtesy Frank Bogert Collection)

Lady," and got the Palm Springs newspaper to buy it. Or the real story behind the walls of **Jim** and **Tammy Faye Bakker**'s compound, the inventory of **Walter Annenberg**'s art collection, the true hypocrisy of **Bob Hope,** the absolute hedonism that was the Racquet Club in its heyday.

Where did it all begin? How can it have gone on so long without the kind of tabloid sensationalism which shaped Hollywood and *Hollywood Babylon,* the great seminal work of **Kenneth Anger,** under-

▲ Dancer Ann Miller poses at poolside in the Palm Springs cheesecake tradition. (Photo courtesy Paul Pospesil Collection)

ground filmmaker? Rejected in Tinseltown, he moved to Paris and published his scandalous tales in France in 1959 in a plain brown wrapper. It was 1965 before a pirate edition arrived in New York, and 1975 before the book officially appeared in the United States, in bowdlerized form. What vast, powerful forces made Palm Springs safe haven for every narcissistic obsession and every wild vice? Why is Palm Springs' history so hidden and suppressed?

Partly, the desert itself provides a natural shield. The great Mt. San Jacinto and neighboring peaks, snow-capped even while the village below sizzles in unnatural heat, surround the Coachella Valley. Overland travel into this barren desert was once fraught with danger. Airplane service into Palm Springs didn't begin until 1945 and wasn't conveniently available until the late fifties. The legendary Hollywood colony of the thirties came by private car or train to get away from it all, literally to hide. It was an arduous trip across windswept, godforsaken sand dunes, on a poor road, over the mountains, in blistering weather, but once they got to Palm Springs it was "anything goes."

Palm Springs was known only to the Cahuilla tribe of Mission Indians until 1885, when **"Judge" John Guthrie McCallum** arrived in search of a cure for his young son's tuberculosis. He was followed by **"Doctor" Welwood Murray,** a displaced pharmacist and botanical experimenter who built the first hotel in Palm Springs.

The catastrophic drought of 1894 to 1905 seemed to wipe out all hope of permanent settlement, but Dr. Murray held on to his Palm Springs Hotel while trying to sell it to every guest who visited. (That's another Palm Springs tradition still practiced today in the intimate private resorts.) The drought ended and **"Mother" Nellie Coffman** arrived to visit in 1908. She fell in love with the desert but found Murray's hotel rather dank and depressing, so she opened her own place across the street, the Desert Inn, which would become a world-class hotel. **Jack Benny** and his side-kick **Rochester** were denied rooms there in 1940 because one was Jewish and the other black.

They and the other Hollywood stars found shelter at El Mirador Hotel, built in 1928 by **Prescott W. Stevens** to accommodate the wild and promiscuous Hollywood crowd. The Desert Inn and some of the other snooty Palm Canyon Drive hotels considered the movie colony people slime. They carried over from the British a judgmental disdain for the entertainment profession.

El Mirador was home, however. Handsome **Frank Bogert,** who would become the "cowboy mayor" of Palm Springs, managed the resort and took publicity photos of the glamorous bad boys and girls. He posed with **Clara Bow,** the "It" girl, who didn't really go to bed with the entire University of Southern California football team (including **John Wayne**), as reported in *Hollywood Babylon*. Clara and the jocks were just friends, although they did play all night. No wonder Clara developed such a fondness for sleeping pills, "for my insomnia."

▲ Clara Bow, the "It" girl, with Frank Bogert. She looks like she wants it, and he looks happy to oblige. (Photo courtesy Frank Bogert Collection)

Unfortunately for Stevens, the stock market crashed in 1929 and El Mirador failed, but it was revived by **Warren Pinney** in 1932, and the party continued. Actor **Ralph Bellamy** and his buddy **Charlie Farrell,** a major star in silent films whose career disintegrated with the coming of talkies because he had a high-pitched nelly voice, were avid tennis players with private homes in Palm Springs who finagled court privileges at El Mirador after the Desert Inn kicked them out. But the paying guests often couldn't get on the court because Farrell and Bellamy were always playing. And when **Marlene Dietrich** complained to the management, Pinney told Charlie and Ralph to beat it.

So they paid $6,000 for two hundred acres of "useless" desert land in the north end of town and used fifty-three acres of it to establish the Racquet Club of Palm Springs, a private members-only hideaway with courts and, eventually, rooms, cottages, a famous bamboo bar, and a notorious reputation. They opened on Christmas Day, 1933, charging

▼ Tony Curtis looks on while Charlie Farrell adjusts the tiara on Janet Leigh's head. Palm Springs is famous for its queens. (Photo courtesy Paul Pospesil Collection)

▲ The fabulous Gabor girls attend a soiree for "the beautiful people only" at Le Valauris restaurant, and remain true divas of Palm Springs nightlife. (Palm Springs Life Collection)

▼ Paulette Goddard with Charlie Chaplin's three sons at the El Mirador. Where was Daddy? (Photo courtesy Frank Bogert Collection)

their Hollywood cronies a dollar each to play on their two courts, built at a cost of $7,500. Frank Bogert came over from El Mirador to manage the Racquet Club in 1940, when it's said that Palm Springs police were unable to investigate a murder because they couldn't get in. "Membership has its privileges." Jack Benny's spoof on this alleged incident ended with the punchline, "Just throw the body over the fence."

Benny often broadcast his national radio show from the Plaza Theater in Palm Springs in the early forties, but not everybody was thrilled. **Culver Nichols,** the Hollywood real estate man who had married Prescott Stevens's daughter Sally and who became the first president of the Palm Springs Chamber of Commerce in 1940, recalls giving Benny an Indian blanket he had to pay for himself. **Bing Crosby** tooted in the 1940 New Year at El Mirador, where he played bartender and was barely able to control the antics of his wife **Dixie Lee,** a legendary drinker portrayed by **Susan Hayward** in the picture *Smash Up* in 1947. **Clark Gable** and **Carole Lombard** were regulars at the Racquet Club until the raucous, fun-loving Carole smashed into a mountain during a World War II bond drive tour. When Gable died in 1960, his remains were placed next to Lombard's at Forest Lawn in Glendale.

The actress **Eadie Adams** (not to be confused with Ernie Kovacs' widow, Edie Adams) was friendly with Lombard and Gable, and **Howard Hughes** once bribed a bandleader with $5,000 to get a date with Eadie, who, with her female friend **Pat McGrath,** started Palm Springs' first lesbian hotel, the Desert Knight. It's still in business and still managed by McGrath, although Eadie died March 13, 1983. **Gloria Swanson** was often seen there, although famous for her brief but flamboyant relationships with men.

Lucille Ball and **Desi Arnaz** arrived in the middle of all of this and became, like **Bob** and **Dolores Hope,** unofficial mayoralty of the desert playground. They were among the first to build at the Thunderbird Country Club and later created in the unknown outskirts of Rancho Mirage a fabulous estate which housed 75 couples in bungalows and featured three swimming pools, a dozen tennis courts, and horseback riding in private canyons. **Art Linkletter** had promoted Rancho Mirage when it was empty sands. The Lucy and Desi estate in 1982 became the most lavish gay-oriented establishment in the world, the

▲ Gloria Swanson in a turban which became one of her standard trademarks along with cigarette holders, red lips, and bevies of hangers-on.

▲ Frank and Barbara at one of his Valentine's Day "Love Ins" for Desert Hospital, where Sinatra sings, even if he can't. (Photo courtesy Paul Pospesil Collection)

New Lost World hotel, with a four-star restaurant, nightly striptease shows in two bars, and a wildly licentious atmosphere.

Frank Sinatra was a continuing presence in these years, during a spate of marriages. He once had to be helped off his knees after collapsing, drunk, at Ruby's Dunes, a popular watering hole on Palm Canyon Drive which is now called Confetti. With **Ava Gardner** (married 1951–1957), he kept a private table at the Cantonese House and engaged in fierce temper tantrums and violent quarrels—yet she remained tenderly affectionate toward the Man to her dying hour. She kept keys to his homes in London, Acapulco, and Palm Springs even after their sexual relationship was long over and Frank had married **Barbara Marx,** a desert model with a long history of former boyfriends, who had married **Zeppo Marx** and moved into Palm Springs society after a career as a Las Vegas showgirl.

◄ Gary Cooper in jodphurs at El Mirador. Was he the straight leading man in Palm Springs, or a regular around Errol Flynn's pool? (Photo courtesy Frank Bogert Collection)

With **Mia Farrow** in February and March of 1968, a jealous Sinatra endured watching her openly dating **John Phillips** of the Mamas and the Papas, who came and went from the Palm Springs compound at all hours. With current wife **Barbara,** Frank has now settled down into the comfortable role of elderly philanthropist of Desert Hospital. But Palm Springs remembers.

February 17 to 24, 1954, brought President **Dwight D. Eisenhower** and his always unsteady wife **Mamie** to Palm Springs for a little golf and winter sunshine, but although Ike wasn't the first president to visit the area (**Harry Truman** once left the Racquet Club in a fit of rage because he'd been spotted by the press indulging in some elbow bending exercises), Eisenhower's trip coincided with the infancy of television and sent images of this desert hideaway into every American home. The city fathers still like Ike, and as for the undying rumors of Mamie's little drinking problem, well, they kept it out of the papers.

More presidents came—in fact every president since Ike has come and most who followed him have stayed, and stayed, at **Walter** and **Leonore Annenberg**'s splendid Sunnylands estate. And wouldn't we like to know what goes on behind those locked gates? The art collection includes Steuben glass pieces, Van Gogh's portrait of the wife of the postmaster of Arles and his *Olive Trees,* Gauguin's *Mother and Daughter,* a ming jade Kuei Pei scepter, Renoir's *The Daughters of Catulle Mendes,* Monet's *Garden,* and of course Andrew Wyeth's 1978 portrait of Annenberg himself.

The Annenbergs broke ground for Sunnylands in 1962 and completed it in 1966. **Richard Nixon** liked it so well that he drafted speeches and taped radio addresses there and hid there during his humiliating downfall in 1974. Nixon had named Annenberg his ambassador to Great Britain, an honor the publisher millionaire never forgot. When the **Shah of Iran** was deposed in 1980, his mother and her retinue of servants, family members, and pets stayed at Sunnylands for months. Frank Sinatra married Barbara Marx there in 1976. And as recently as 1990, Annenberg has been writing from Sunnylands in defense of his old pal Bob Hope, whose offer to "donate" land in the Santa Monica mountains to the National Park Service has been called self-serving and hypocritical. "The frequent discouragement philanthropists learn is that no good deed may go unpunished," Annen-

▲ Did Mamie have a little unsteadiness in her gait? (Photo courtesy Paul Pospesil Collection)

berg wrote in the letters column of the *Los Angeles Times*. If you want to write back, his address is P. O. Box 98, Rancho Mirage, CA 92270.

The 205-acre walled compound with barbed wire and oleander and eucalyptus landscaping has a private golf course and a security system that would be the envy of many heads of state. When **George Bush** and Japanese prime minister **Toshiki Kaifu** arrived for their 1990 summit, they limoed away from Palm Springs Airport heading for Annenberg's place, leaving Mayor **Sonny Bono** and his wife **Mary** standing on the tarmac, diplomatically excluded despite her Donna Karan suit and his outsized sunglasses.

Liberace arrived in Palm Springs in 1952 and introduced new levels of decadence to the old whore of a town that had seen everything, or thought it had. "Lee's" television show started that year and ran through 1956. The Chi Chi Club, which had been the place for many late-night bacchanals in the thirties and forties, had fallen into disrepair and was for sale. Lee fantasized about buying it and operating it as a private club where he and his friends would play for free and socialize, according to his longtime publicist **Jamie James.**

After owning several smaller houses in town, Liberace ended up buying the 1925 Cloisters estate on Alejo Road, built as a private mansion and later used as a thirty-two-room hotel. He celebrated New Year's Eve of 1968 there with James and other friends. The asking price for the house was $210,000, but Liberace actually paid $185,000 ("he considered it too cheap to pass up," James said) and then spent $136,000 to fix it up. It was in bad repair, and Lee renovated it to its former posh grandeur.

By 1960, the Desert Inn had been torn down and replaced by a shopping plaza, continuing the trend of new business and glamor moving "down valley" to Palm Desert, Rancho Mirage, and Indian Wells, out of the city limits of Palm Springs. Liberace stayed at the Cloisters, however, carrying on outrageous parties and liaisons with young men until his death from AIDS on February 4, 1987.

The Cloisters was opened for press viewing on March 28, 1990, and revealed a lifestyle of pure opulence tainted with the kitschy bad taste of an old queen and the decline of a neighborhood once considered exclusive. The house is across the street from a Catholic church, Our

---

▶ Liberace's great loves, aside from his boyfriends, included the dogs he called his "babies." (Photo courtesy Paul Pospesil Collection)

Lady of Solitude, where sandwiches are passed out daily to the homeless who loiter in the vicinity. Inside, Liberace's toilet is a throne, with armrests and a high back done up in red velvet. The shower curtain features replicas of Michaelangelo's David, while the wallpaper is decorated with Greek couples fucking in every imaginable position. There is a **Gloria Vanderbilt** suite, a **Rudolph Valentino** room (Liberace's middle name was Valentino, and the Great Lover was an early Palm Springs celebrity who made several pictures here in the twenties), a room wallpapered in tiger skin, a Marie Antoinette suite, a bath with mirrored walls and ceiling and a pool-sized Jacuzzi, and a collection of strange bric-a-brac and junk no thrift shop could unload, including plastic birthday cakes and a life-size stuffed male doll with erect penis.

Into this world he introduced his young escorts, took his pills, and kept his cranky mother. The most touching items in the house were his enormous early-technology television screen and gigantic first-generation videotape machine, which he used to watch his vast collection of explicit gay films. But the porn collection itself is gone, vanished like a desert mirage.

The **Kennedys** were well known and visible in Palm Springs in the sixties. Frank Sinatra supplied **JFK** with Hollywood starlets, while **Peter Lawford** did the same for Frank. Sinatra had been instrumental in helping Kennedy win the 1960 election, but he was enraged when JFK finally came to Palm Springs March 24 to 26, 1962, and stayed at Republican singer Bing Crosby's house instead. It was left to Peter Lawford to break the news to Sinatra, who never again considered Lawford a friend.

Bobby Kennedy was trying to dismantle the Mafia at the time. Palm Springs was known as a safe haven for the Mob, and Sinatra's house in particular had offered hospitality to notorious gangsters such as **Sam Giancana,** who shared a mistress (**Judith Campbell**) with Kennedy. (The would-be Kennedy mansion was eventually rechristened the Agnew House in 1969, when Frank developed a close friendship with Nixon's vice president **Spiro Agnew**—who is locally remembered for opening a speech, "It's nice to be here in Palm Beach.")

Illegal but sanctioned gambling clubs had operated over the town line in neighboring Cathedral City throughout the twenties and thirties, until the U.S. Army shut them down during World War II. The most famous of these were the Dunes Club, run by **Al Wertheimer** of the Detroit mob, which had a peephole in its massive front door, a huge bar in dark woods and red velvets, and a menu featuring only Kansas steak and Maine lobster, and the 139 Club, a plain plywood dive serving chili and beans and free drinks.

The current mayor of Cathedral City, **George Hardie,** is also a minority share owner and managing partner of the Bicycle Club, a legal card parlor in Bell Gardens, a rundown Los Angeles suburb, and was defeated in a 1989 referendum effort to gain permission to build a similar gambling club in the desert. In March, 1990, his associate **Benjamin "Barry" Kramer,** was convicted of laundering drug money used to build the card club, and the federal government seized the operation, touted as the world's largest poker parlor, on April 3, 1990. Hardie claims ignorance and innocence of Mafia ties and the drug trade, and his investor group's 35 percent of the casino was released by the government.

Lyndon Johnson met with Mexican president **Adolfo López Mateos** in Palm Springs in 1964 to settle the Mexico-Texas border dispute, and Richard Nixon was a frequent visitor, but it remained for **Jerry** and **Betty Ford** to make the kind of impression on the town that Ike and Mamie had, and for somewhat similar reasons. Betty of course was so strung out on booze and drugs that her family staged an "intervention," which led to her hospitalization and recovery and the subsequent founding of the Betty Ford Center, dedicated October 3, 1982, at the Eisenhower Medical Center in Rancho Mirage. Whereas Mamie was widely suspected to be a drunk but managed to keep it under wraps, Betty copped to it publicly and enhanced her own fame with books and speaking engagements on the new industry of helping people get off the sauce. She doesn't discourage people from trying to get well for free at A.A. meetings, but in her book *Betty, A Glad Awakening,* she pushes the advantages of her more expensive private-hospital treatment. Of course, many of the celebrities who dried out at her center later went back to drugs and bottles.

Palm Springs may not be the best place in the world to recover from bad habits. The town is dedicated to the pursuit of mindless pleasures. One of Betty's clients, and one of Palm Springs' most famous nogoodniks, was defrocked evangelist **Jim Bakker**—although Bakker appears to have joined the program primarily to support his wife, **Tammy Faye,** who had a serious substance-abuse problem. The stories about Jim and Tammy Faye are still circulating around the desert.

They were both highly visible in town as well as in the media. When the accusation that Jim was homosexual began to emerge in 1987, he denied it repeatedly, but the fact is Bakker was well known within the gay community and was seen attending gay functions such as the whipped cream wrestling at Daddy Warbuck's, a notorious Cathedral City transvestite-oriented nightclub, and "Leather Night" at the C. C. Construction Company, a leather bar. His indiscretions were legendary. As for Tammy Faye, she bought her famous eyelashes at the Thrifty Discount Store on Palm Canyon Drive for $1.98 a pair, and the manager there will gladly show you the brands she favored. Tammy oozed up and down the shopping district, a familiar sight in her garish outfits and streaking mascara. **Armistead Maupin,** the gay novelist, joked about Jim Bakker with the comment, "What self respecting gay man would let his wife get messed up with all that makeup?"

The Bakkers violated the principal law of Palm Springs. They let their dirty laundry show in public. From Greenbriar Lane in Palm Desert, where they had a $430,000 house, they moved into a $600,000 Palm Springs compound that was always surrounded by reporters and cameras. Tammy Faye made a game of leaving the house in disguise to foil the press. The Bakkers' neighbor, **Lilli Marzliker,** found the whole circus less than amusing, especially after giving $25,000 of her own savings in sincere donations to the PTL—known in Palm Springs to stand for "Pay for Tammy's Lashes." But the flamboyant couple did bring the town back into the limelight in the eighties.

As did **Sonny Bono,** the current mayor and former male bimbo of Sonny and Cher and "I Got You, Babe" fame. While most observers agree that Sonny's talent career ended with his divorce from **Cher,** he regained worldwide attention by successfully running for celebrity-mayor of Palm Springs, comparing himself to **Clint Eastwood,** who won election in Carmel in 1986. "Comparing Sonny to Clint," snorted former mayor Frank Bogert, "is like comparing chicken shit to chicken salad."

But nobody can deny Sonny's sincerity as he attempts to restore Palm Springs to some of its former grandeur. He is faced with major problems, including deteriorating neighborhoods, increasing crime and homelessness, and a high retail vacancy rate on the main shopping drag, Palm Canyon Drive. He and his wife Mary are both teetotalers and born-again Christians, but that doesn't stop them from selling drinks to the tourists at Bono's Racquet Club Restaurant and Mary's Nightclub. Sonny's ideas for rebuilding Palm Springs are aimed at getting the tourists to come back from the newer, flashier resorts down valley such as the Ritz Carlton in Rancho Mirage or the Marriot's Desert Springs, with the world's largest man-made lake, in Palm Desert. Sonny wants to popularize an annual Palm Springs Film Festival—the first one in January 1990 was an embarrassment that failed to produce the hoped-for celebrity visitors—and a Grand Prix–type motorcar race through the streets of the village.

Sonny addressed the membership of the Desert Business Association at a banquet on October 17, 1989, the night of the catastrophic San Francisco earthquake. Seventy-five or eighty people bowed their heads in the Mesquite Country Club dining room as he called for a moment of silence—to honor the recent passing of **Bette Davis.** It was a perfectly Palm Springs moment, an exercise in desert imbecility, as we all mourned Miss Bette while listening to the television in the adjacent bar blaring news of "thousands feared dead in massive San Francisco earthquake."

His dinner speech then focused on the growing problem of Spring Break in Palm Springs, that annual mayhem which brings hordes of high school and college students swarming over the streets, determined to raise hell. "They just get deliriously drunk, and we just can't control them," Sonny complained, adding that he was considering closing the main street to thwart the cruising activity. (This brought howls of protests from local residents who said that closing the main drag would just send the reveling throngs into the smaller side streets.)

But Sonny Bono has done one thing for Palm Springs, which is to reestablish its standing as Babylon reincarnated after a slow period in the seventies and eighties. His cartoon T-shirt, "I Want You, Babe—Meet Me in Palm Springs," has raised over $17,000 for the beleaguered city treasury—although he spent a whole day in April 1990 patroling the main drag asking merchants to remove "obscene" or offensive T-shirts from their windows. (These included messages such as "Lick It—Slam It—Suck It"

"Big Peckers Club," and "Jump My Bones." Some said the Bono T-shirt was the most obscene of all.) He complains about the motorcycle gangs in town but rides around on a black Harley Davidson, dispensing frontier justice. He clearly understands the value of T-shirts, if not the politics of responsible municipal management. And T-shirt shops are the only businesses making money in downtown Palm Springs today.

Frederick Loewe, composer of *My Fair Lady, Gigi, Brigadoon, Camelot,* and other hit musicals, died in Palm Springs on February 14, 1988, and now at last the true story of **Baroness Anna Maria von Steiner** has come out. "Madame von Steiner" was allegedly a world-famous concert pianist and teacher from Dresden, Germany, who first appeared in Palm Springs in 1972 for a widely publicized visit with Loewe, pianists **Earl Wild** and **Van Cliburn,** and opera singer **Lily Pons.** The newspaper coverage was lavish, with a full page story and photographs. But Anna Maria von Steiner was an elaborate fraud, a local singer and interior decorator named Allan Keller, done up in drag.

Keller, now 74 and known as "the Perle Mesta of Palm Springs" for his extravagant parties, chuckled as he remembered the incident. "We had a good time with Anna Maria for about three years," he said. "We even had her listed in the *Palm Springs Gold Book* and she got invited to all the best social affairs. This town has always been crazy for titles and most of them are phony anyway. We have a **Baron** and **Baroness d'Zamant** in town, and people say it started because his first name was Baron. Who knows about the **Gabor** sisters?"

"Madame Steiner performed for a select group at Dr. Loewe's magnificent estate in Palm Springs," wrote "Latitia Kountz," music editor of the *Desert Times* of Palm Springs. "He [Loewe] reminisced about the first concert he heard Anna Steiner play in Vienna . . . when he was a small child. 'If I live to be one hundred and fifty, I will never fail to recall the salubrious effect of this musical giant on my life and career. Her image, deep in my past, became the blueprint for *My Fair Lady*.' "

Keller, who claims to be the "only man in town who's had a mastectomy," was honored for his contributions to cultural causes at a testimonial dinner on December 3, 1989, attended by 350 leading Palm Springs personalities. His house parties have accommodated more peo-

◄ Mary and Sonny have made a tidy living selling drinks to the tourists. (Photo courtesy Paul Pospesil Collection)

ple than that, including special tributes to Lily Pons, Andre Previn, Perry Como, Joli Gabor, Merv Griffin, Barbara Sinatra, Renata Scotto and Hal Wallis. They always ended with a floor show starring Keller as a bosomy femme fatale. He owns a **Helen Rose** gown that was on display in April 1990 at the gift shop in the Racquet Club, touted as "an original design work by a famous star in a well known picture," without more specific identification.

The Racquet Club has fallen on hard times. It's on the market for $10 million, certainly a good return on the $6,000 that Charlie Farrell and Ralph Bellamy invested in 1933, but there are no takers at that price despite swirling rumors of unnamed Hollywood producers who allegedly want to make a TV miniseries about the heyday of the club. The current owner, **M. Larry Lawrence,** who salvaged the Hotel del Coronado in San Diego, held a press conference on March 24, 1990, to boast of his own successes, but it's obvious to Palm Springs insiders that the Racquet Club is not what it used to be, since it began soliciting nonmembers for restaurant meals and room reservations last year, for the first time in its history.

The Clark Gable Cottage (#61) was dedicated in March 1990 by **John Clark Gable,** who was born four months after his father's death in 1960, but most of the Racquet Club's clientele is now geriatric. The current membership list includes, **Jack Paar** (born in 1918), **Ernest Borgnine** (1917), **Ricardo Montalban** (1920), **Johnny Carson** (1925), and of course original founder Ralph Bellamy (1904). "Famous guests" sighted at the club in March 1990 were **Caesar Romero** (1907), **Anne Jeffreys** (1923), and relative youngsters **Chubby Checker** (born in 1941, and registered under a pseudonym) and **Julie Newmar** (born in 1935, and oddly enough described in the club newsletter as "seen in the dining room, putting to rest the rumor of her demise"). Palm Springs is sometimes called "God's Waiting Room" because so many come here to die. Lately it's called "Home of the Gay Nineties, since everyone is either gay or in their nineties."

Founder Charlie Farrell, who made his last comeback in TV's "My Little Margie" series as a summer replacement for "I Love Lucy" in 1952, died in 1990. (Charlie was headed for Europe as a guest of New York banker **Ben Mayer** in May 1952 when **Hal Roach** called him in for the "Margie" show. It was so successful that he got his own "Charlie

▲ An elderly Mary Martin does the boogaloo with Jack Paar, 1979. (Photo courtesy Paul Pospesil Collection)

Farrell Show" in the summer of 1956.) Farrell's own father died at 96 in the nearby Indio Convalescent Home.

Gone are the days when **Rock Hudson** and his bride **Phyllis Gates** (married from November 1955 to April 1958) used to hang around at the Racquet Club and waterski on the Salton Sea. Rock later became a Palm Springs regular, staying at the home of his personal secretary **Mark Miller** in Palm Desert. Knowing Hudson was dying of AIDS, Miller brought him to the desert, in hopes of covering it up in the best Palm Springs tradition. Hudson's estranged ex-manager and former lover **Tom Clark** is also here, embroiled in a libel suit with **Marc Christian.**

Gone forever are the studio shoots by the Racquet Club pool, where photographer **Bruno Bernard** of Hollywood "discovered" **Norma Jean Baker (Marilyn Monroe)** and "everybody was on a party all the time," as Bellamy said. Oldtimers remember the day sizzling starlet **Lupe Velez** stripped naked and swam laps in the pool, and the night **Peter**

Lorre and **Gilbert Roland** and their wives demanded that dinner be served in the pool—and were obliged. No more are the nights around the bamboo bar with **Spencer Tracy, Jean Harlow, Errol Flynn, Rita Hayworth, Douglas Fairbanks, Joan Crawford, Mary Pickford, John Barrymore,** and **Greer Garson** vying for one another's attentions. Spencer Tracy's cottage is now the maintenance shed. Greer Garson's last appearance was at the 1984 Easter services at Palm Desert Presbyterian Church, reading from the New Testament in her famously dignified intonations: "He is risen, he is not here!"

PALM SPRINGS RISES again every Easter season, when the crazed young revelers of Spring Break clog the streets with their uninhibited party-till-you-drop public riots. It rises, too, in the persons of younger celebrities like folk singer **Donovan** and actress **Diahann Carroll,** who are hiding out in the High Desert mountains, and it sings from the top of San Jacinto the sun-worshiper's anthem. Spring brings the return of blazing desert sunshine to the town famous for the best weather in the United States, the hot spot of the world, the place where wearing nothing is socially correct and Hollywood is only ninety miles away, near enough to run from but far enough to hide from.

Palm Springs' only world-class distinction is that it has always provided and always will provide an environment in which absolute hedonism is not only possible but inevitable. Lacking industry, it knows no work ethic. Lacking history, it has kept its dirty secrets hidden. Only now, when the pioneers are old and outspoken as children and many of the principals are dead, are the true stories coming forth.

I was drawn here like a moth to the flames of that desert sun, one small person devoted to the idea of a life of ease after growing up in Massachusetts, struggling with Washington and New York, traveling the world in search of a voice, wading through cold Seattle rainstorms, inching closer in Carmel and Monterey and Hollywood sublets, finally arriving at forty-four in this cauldron of hidden murder and vacant excess, and the only way I can justify my slothful surrender is to tell it like it is, to burn down the house. For tales from hidden Babylon, read on.

▶ The divine Marilyn was "discovered" by agent Johnny Hyde at the Racquet Club. Hyde left his wife and children for Marilyn, but shortly thereafter had a fatal heart attack at the club. (Photo courtesy Star File)

In the Beginning

PALM SPRINGS WASN'T MUCH of anything before the current century, although the Cahuilla band of Agua Caliente Indians inhabited the place for thousands of years, living on dates from the palm trees, acorns and other nuts, and mesquite beans, used to make flour and tortillas. They retreated to the hillside canyons to escape the summer heat and drew from the natural hot springs in the winter. These sacred springs are now walled inside the Spa Hotel in downtown Palm Springs, but the Indians retain ownership and collect a lease fee. The tribe owns half of Palm Springs, from a federal grant in 1877. The hotel—faded grandeur—once hosted Hollywood's fast set but by 1991 was under new ownership seeking a new clientele.

The Indians might be better able to make a profit managing the place. They do very well at their legal desert gambling spots, the horse race satellite palace in Indio and the Morongo Indian Bingo games on Interstate 10 (top prize, half a million dollars).

But the white man arrived and chased the Indians off their own land, as usual. It started with "Judge" John Guthrie McCallum in 1885, believed to be the first white settler. He was never really a judge, but in Palm Springs you can give yourself any title you like. He was actually

◄ Starlets convene at the Palm Springs train depot in the 1930s. This shot was posed by Frank Bogert to publicize the burgeoning desert resort. (Photo courtesy Frank Bogert Collection)

a minor politician in Oakland and a U.S. Indian agent in San Bernardino when he migrated into the blistering desert seeking a climate that would cure his son's tuberculosis. McCallum's homestead was originally 320 acres, bought for $150 from the Indian Pedro Chino. The judge opened the first general store in the desert and persuaded another adventurer, "Doctor" Welwood Murray, to build the first hotel.

Murray, as you've already guessed, was no doctor. He was an agricultural researcher from Scotland. But he hired a local Indian to dress up like an Arabian shiek and ride a camel out to the railroad stop seven miles away, passing out brochures to lure travelers into the new paradise. It worked pretty well. His Palm Springs Hotel guests included naturalist John Muir, author Helen Hunt Jackson, and U.S. Vice President Charles Fairbanks. The good doctor made a practice of trying to sell the property to everyone who stayed there. That's still going on in Palm Springs.

Credit Murray, though, with understanding the recreational and resort value of a place that was otherwise useless sand and sun. He was followed by Nellie Coffman, who built the Desert Inn in 1908, and Pearl McCallum McManus, the judge's daughter, who built the Oasis in 1924. In 1925, Nellie put in the first swimming pool in town. Today, of course, Palm Springs is swollen with hotel rooms, and there is one pool for every four residents. It's possible, but miserably unlucky, to live without one.

The Hollywood stars began arriving very early on, in the days of silent pictures and two-reel comedies. Fatty Arbuckle was a favorite local winter resident who rented a bungalow at the Desert Inn for the entire season. Arbuckle's career was jettisoned after "he stuck a Coke bottle up a girl's snatch, and she died," said former Palm Springs mayor Frank Bogert. The girl was actress Virginia Rappe, a well known Hollywood hussy, and there has long been some disagreement about what kind of foreign object damaged her bladder. Fatty was acquitted of the crime, but his career in pictures and at the Desert Inn was over. He was remembered for his prodigious drinking bouts.

Rudolph Valentino used the desert landscape to advantage in his movies and was photographed visiting the famous Palm Springs hermit, Peter Pender, who went about naked in public. Peter and Rudy seemed to have a lot to say to each other. Rudy was another one who denied liking guys, but Palm Springs looked the other way, didn't notice. Palm Springs was safe.

Another myth that's being actively perpetuated for profit is the famous story of Al Capone at Two Bunch Palms in Desert Hot Springs. The resort is supposedly where Capone holed up in 1932 to hide from the Feds, and the hotel management today proudly points out the bullet holes, gun tower, secret doorways, and other relics of Capone's stay. In 1990, that Capone story was recreated one more time, for the official Two Bunch Palms tourist brochure. But it's purely a lie. The truth is Capone was safely tucked away in jail when he was said to be at Two Bunch Palms. Nobody in Palm Springs lets the truth get in the way of making a buck off the tourists, however.

▼ Frank Bogert in the annual Desert Circus parade, a perennial entertainment. (Photo courtesy Frank Bogert Collection)

▲ Governor Pat Brown cuts the ribbon on the inaugural ride of the Palm Springs Aerial Tramway, 1963. (Photo courtesy Paul Pospesil Collection)

World War II had no adverse effect on Palm Springs—in fact, the desert movie colony boomed with unprecedented prosperity. The El Mirador was transformed into an army hospital, and General George Patton trained his regiments on the sand-blown desert. The addition of thousands of servicemen to the local scene guaranteed high times for the bars, hotels, prostitutes, and after-hours clubs. The illegal casinos in Cathedral City were closed down after the police chief mysteriously disappeared, but Palm Springs was still a major safe asylum for the Mob. Hoodlums and petty criminals from Las Vegas came to cool off in the hot town. More than one dead body has conveniently vanished in the desert. And law enforcement depended on who was paying.

Frank Sinatra, Dean Martin, Sammy Davis, Jr., Peter Lawford, and other members of the Rat Pack became familiar fixtures in Palm

Springs in the fifties and sixties. Lucille Ball and Desi Arnaz, William and Mousie Powell, Dinah Shore, Elvis himself, and of course Bob Hope all muscled into the scene. Bobby Kennedy tried to rub out the Mafia in Palm Springs, but he got his at the Ambassador Hotel in L.A. Even now, in the "Gay Nineties," one hears stories, one sees goons in high places, and then, just as suddenly, they're gone.

One could tell you stories if one were leaving town on the 9:18 to Yuma.

▼ Barbara Sinatra, left, in her early career as a model and desert playgirl. (Photo courtesy Gail B. Thompson Collection)

► Harpo's got his hands full at the El Mirador Hotel. So did brother Zeppo when he married Barbara (later Mrs. Frank Sinatra). (Photo courtesy Paul Pospesil Collection)

Charlie Farrell

Some Kind of Raquet

WHEN CHARLIE FARRELL, UNDENIABLY the father of Palm Springs decadence, died on May 6, 1990, even the local press didn't take notice for a week. Pushing ninety, Farrell had stayed home, alone except for nurse Mildred Gamache, watching television in bed and spurning company for years. "Mr. Palm Springs," the soul of conviviality, Founder of the Racquet Club, former mayor, star of the silent screen and TV's "My Little Margie," ended life a reclusive desert rat.

Born Charles David Farrell in Walpole, Massachusetts, on August 9, 1900, he thrilled the nation in the silent picture *Seventh Heaven,* costarring Janet Gaynor, in 1927. Farrell and Gaynor made a number of other movies together, including *Sunnyside Up* and *Street Angel,* but Charlie's popularity as a sex symbol crashed when the talkies came in.

So Charlie retired from films to spend his time and money playing tennis, staying up all night drinking and carousing, and fucking the many starlets who came to Palm Springs. His great passion was tennis, and he and his buddy Ralph Bellamy opened the Racquet Club of Palm Springs, which went on to become an exclusive membership club attracting Gloria Swanson, William Powell, Judy Garland, Bing Crosby, Joan Fontaine, Rudy Vallee, Cary Grant, Rock Hudson, Douglas Fair-

◄ Janet Gaynor and Charlie Farrell, co-stars of *Seventh Heaven,* unintentionally wore identical clown costumes to the Big Top Ball, or so the P.S. story goes. (Photo courtesy Frank Bogert Collection)

banks, Bob Hope, Clara Bow, Marilyn Monroe, Erroll Flynn, Al Jolson, Paulette Goddard—the list is endless. "Everyone wanted to play, but nobody wanted to pay," Charlie complained.

It wasn't long before the Racquet Club became the "in" place in Palm Springs, the favored spot for drinking all night, playing musical bedrooms, and hiding Hollywood secrets from the press. The more conservative Palm Springs hotels, including the Ingleside Inn and the Desert Inn, discriminated against Jews and blacks, while the Racquet Club welcomed both. (Mel Haber, current owner of the Ingleside Inn, reported that when he bought the hotel, he found old records of reservations in which the letter *J* was entered alongside the names of Jewish guests.)

Charlie preferred Old Rarity Scotch, drank for days on end without eating, spent all night at the illegal casinos in Cathedral City and returned to the Racquet Club at dawn, still dressed in a fancy white suit, where manager Frank Bogert would "push him in the pool, get him in the steam bath, sober him up and get him in bed."

He shared his bed with his wife, actress Virginia Valli (née McSweeney), countless other women, and likely a few men. "Ginny," who died September 24, 1968, apparently tolerated Charlie's well-known extramarital adventures, while she managed the club and prevented Charlie from pissing away his investments. She was dowdy and conservative, but a good interior designer and a savvy judge of real estate. Charlie and Ginny got filthy rich in desert real estate after their movie careers had long fizzled out.

Perhaps because of the high voice and his habit of kissing everyone who entered the Racquet Club, men included, Charlie was often suspected of having gay liaisons. He didn't admit to it publicly. William Gargan once called Charlie a fairy in the Racquet Club bar, and Farrell knocked him down with a single punch. Bartender Tex Gregg claimed that Gargan apologized to Farrell, and the two men went on drinking, arms around each other, and became fast friends.

Ralph Bellamy sold his share of the club back to the Farrells after a couple of years of managing it while Charlie made films in England. During his brief stint as manager, Bellamy was hoodwinked by dishonest bartenders and waiters who pocketed the receipts from the jam-packed bamboo bar until the state Board of Equalization hit the Racquet Club

▲ Cary Grant, of course, another of Palm Springs' ambiguous gentleman callers, and a Racquet Club regular. (Photo Courtesy Paul Pospesil Collection)

for $48,000 in unpaid liquor taxes. He once brought in a "casino night" entertainment whose roulette wheel was so crooked the magnets pulled the hairpins off one lady's coiffure. And he befriended Al Wertheimer, a member of Detroit's Purple Gang, who owned and managed the highly illegal Dunes Club gambling joint over the town line in Cathedral City.

The Racquet Club was exclusive in a highly arbitrary sense. Farrell understood the value of importing young, undiscovered talent to mingle with the heavyweight stars, producers, and other rich players. Anybody Charlie liked could get into the club; anybody he disliked could not. And he liked Norma Jean Baker, who came to be Marilyn Monroe.

The divine MM met Hollywood agent Johnny Hyde at the Racquet Club in 1948, and he more or less launched her career. Hyde (born Haidabura) was fifty-three years old at the time, married to Mozelle Cravens, father of four sons, and representing top stars such as Bob Hope, Lana Turner, and Rita Hayworth. Marilyn was a nubile 22. Hyde fell madly in love with her, made a complete fool of himself over her, left his wife and family, and arranged cosmetic nose and chin surgery for Marilyn in 1950. His infatuation with the blonde bombshell did in his ailing ticker; Johnny Hyde suffered a heart attack at the Racquet Club on December 17, 1950, and died the following day.

Darryl F. Zanuck, head of Twentieth Century Fox, also met Marilyn in Palm Springs, when Joseph Schenck of MGM brought her around to his house. Zanuck gave the starlet her first role, in *The Asphalt Jungle*. In January, 1954, Marilyn and Joe DiMaggio spent their honeymoon in the area, mostly tucked away playing billiards in a cabin up in the Idyllwild Hills. And Marilyn returned to Palm Springs on March 24, 1962, to share the bed of President John F. Kennedy at Bing Crosby's home.

The Racquet Club carried on, and on. Charlie took a liking to polo and built the PS Polo Field, which was known locally as Farrell's Folly. Clever Charlie managed to dump it on naive singing cowboy Gene Autry, however, as a spring training home for his California Angels and summer ballpark for the minor league Palm Springs Angels.

Ginger Rogers and high-powered Hollywood attorney Gregson Bautzer met at the Racquet Club and promptly became a popular couple there, ending Bautzer's volatile relationship with Joan Crawford, who posed by the club pool wearing a lynx coat and leading a poodle and

Bautzer on a constant leash. Meat merchant Jack Freeman, who delivered hamburgers to the club, recalled a monumental Sunday morning fight between Crawford and the dapper Gregson. They'd been up all Saturday night drinking, and Joan was screaming filthy obscenities, dressed only in a flimsy robe. When she took a broad swing at Bautzer's chin, both of her breasts flopped out. Ginger Rogers kept Greg out of Joan's way while Crawford threw a tantrum, but Bautzer went on to other women when he tired of Ginger, and finally drank himself into an early and ugly death. Ginger and Jacques Bergerac burst into the Racquet Club on a sunny Saturday afternoon in 1954, and she announced, "We did it! We're married!" "Let's have a party," said Charlie.

Producer Hal Roach dreamed up the "My Little Margie" TV show at the Racquet Club in 1952 and asked Charlie to come out of retirement and play spoiled-rich-girl Gale Storm's father in the series. It was a second career in show business for Farrell, who hadn't landed a film role since 1942 and was a forgotten man in Hollywood. But Charlie was perfect as the fussy, irascible Vernon Albright.

He and Gale Storm, always arguing on screen, also disliked each other intensely off the set. When offered a stage tour with Storm, Farrell declined flatly. Gale was difficult to get along with. But "My Little Margie," originally a summer fill-in for the "I Love Lucy" show, was a big hit and lasted through 150 episodes from 1952 to 1955. After that, Charlie got his own show, "The Charles Farrell Show," from 1956 to 1960. It was a sitcom based on a sanitized version of what went on at the Racquet Club. If the true bedroom antics were recorded, Charlie said, "We'd all be in San Quentin or divorced."

Bing Crosby got stinko in the Racquet Club with some regularity. His trademark prank was taking a bottle of Glenlivet Scotch and pouring some into every glass on the bar, regardless of what people were drinking, all the while belting out a song. Debbie Reynolds tried to crash the club stage, but Charlie didn't want her to entertain. She honeymooned with Eddie Fisher at the club but never forgave Charlie.

President Harry Truman, of course a Democrat and union supporter, once walked through a picket line of the Culinary Workers Union to get into the Racquet Club. Charlie was not overly impressed by high-ranking officials. He even forgot Mamie Eisenhower's name while both

▲ Actress Jane Russell and Bob Waterfield at the Racquet Club. (Photo courtesy Paul Pospesil Collection)

were loaded to the tits. He called her "dear" instead. Prince Philip of Britain arrived in the middle of a wild Peppermint Twist party.

The Farrells sold the Racquet Club in 1959 for $1.2 million, carrying back 80 percent of the mortgage themselves, with Charlie staying on as chairman of the board and principal drunk. The new owner, Robert Morton of Pasadena, was so unpopular with his employees that, when somebody accidentally locked him in the steam room, people suspected an attempted murder. Morton escaped unharmed after two hours.

The Racquet Club changed hands again in 1964, by which time Charlie was fed up with it. It became a pale shadow of its riotous past. "The whole mystique of the Racquet Club was because of Charlie," said Palm Springs TV social editor Gloria Greer. "The moment he left, it just died. There will never be anything like that around here again."

Farrell stayed home in his bathrobe, watching TV night and day, as he descended into senility and decrepitude. In the end, he couldn't recognize his playboy buddies and best friends. When he died, nobody heard about it until long after he was buried without services, alongside Ginny, in Welwood Murray Memorial Park. You can't get in there; it's locked and gated.

Culver Nichols, Pioneer

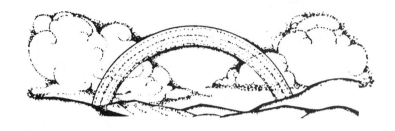

ULVER NICHOLS HAS BEEN living for fifty-seven years in the same north end Palm Springs house, tucked invisibly away behind a rural mail box and dirt road in a thickly landscaped area behind Desert Hospital. He was President of the Palm Springs Chamber of Commerce in the year 1940, when it incorporated.

Interviewed in 1990, Culver said:

The Chamber of Commerce existed long before 1940. In 1932 it was already called the Chamber. It was not incorporated, and the city was not incorporated yet. The secretary-manager was Frank "Pops" Shannon. He was the owner of a small apartment house just around the corner from the Desert Inn, owned and operated by Nellie Coffman. She started it as Nellie's Boarding House, and it became a world destination hotel. She started with little tent houses. Dr. Coffman was her husband, Earl was her son, and he became the father of Betty Kieley, who married Tom Kieley. Tom worked at the Desert Inn.

This was a little old village. Everybody knew everybody else and their personal affairs. I joined the Chamber during Shannon's reign, and I had a real estate agency. I came here from Hollywood and had property there. I was the second realtor in town. Harold Hicks was the first. His son is Jim Hicks, who was also a president of the Chamber.

Palm Springs is wealthy in its people. It's the character and drive of our people that made Palm Springs. Palm Springs is liberally endowed by nature with all the amenities waiting to be exploited. The physical setting is out of this world. Everyone who comes to Palm Springs comes back. It's a wonderful experience approaching this warm, friendly oasis at the foot of the magnificent mountain. The place develops its men and women to match its mountains. The warmth and friendship of the people goes with the warmth of the desert, embracing all.

I sold homes to some Hollywood celebrities. Ask around— were the film people welcomed with open arms here or did they encounter some difficulty getting into hotels? We carried over the British prejudice against the theatrical profession. *Lost Horizon* was shot here in the thirties but people didn't want to admit it. Frank Bogert welcomed the stars from the north end of town, at El Mirador. Also the Hollywood industry was partly Jewish and there was still some prejudice in those days. Jack Benny came here and brought Rochester, but he couldn't get into any of the downtown hotels. They stayed at El Mirador.

I got the lot (where the Chamber building is) from Auntie Pearl McManus. It may have taken me six months of negotiation, because she had these migraine headaches. She was a real loner, married to Austen but she wore the pants. Her property is an important part of our history.

I was president a number of different times in the thirties and forties. The Chamber operated on a shoestring. When Jack Benny did his first broadcast from our Plaza Theater of his national radio show, the Chamber showed its appreciation by presenting him with an Indian blanket which I purchased at Indianoya for $25. And I paid for it myself. He showed more shock and surprise than pleasure but he draped it over his arm and wore it through the warmup for the show.

Yes, I'm optimistic for the future of the city. It has everything. Location. The mountains shelter us from the raw coastal climate. Palm Springs has the special charm of a place first settled by the Indians, who owned and used the hot springs, seeds, nuts, animals. They have a fine tribal organization and their own planning commission.

I was considered a figure to be reckoned with in the north side of town. The Desert Inn was the ruling factor in the center, and the south belonged to Pearl McManus and her husband. My father-in-law, Prescott T. Stevens, was a pioneer here. His daughter and I were childhood sweethearts in Hollywood.

Who's Got It?

Wealthiest People in Palm Springs

1 – Walter Annenberg, age 82, Rancho Mirage: $1.65 billion

2 – Marvin Davis, age 65, Rancho Mirage: $1.65 billion

3 – Edward J. DeBartolo, age 81, Palm Springs: $1.4 billion

4 – Ewing Kauffman, age 74, Indian Wells: $835 million

5 – Cargill MacMillan, Jr., age 63, Indian Wells: $730 million

◄ Leonore and Walter Annenberg, the desert's version of unofficial royalty, richer than Croesus. (Photo courtesy Paul Pospesil Collection)

6 – William Clay Ford, age 76, Palm Springs: $610 million

7 – Alexander "Gus" Spanos, age 67, Indian Wells: $600 million

8 – M. Larry Lawrence, age 64, Palm Springs: $400 million

9 – Gene Autry, age 83, Palm Springs: $300 million

10 – George Argyros, age 53, Palm Springs: $290 million

Source: Forbes 400 list, 1990.

The Mob
and
the Dunes

Wide Open Spaces in Little Vegas

FUNNY HOW MANY PEOPLE knew about it, how blatantly illegal it was, and how long it prospered. Casino gambling was a big part of the lure of Palm Springs in the thirties and forties, even if the joints themselves were discreetly placed in barren Cathedral City, just over the town line.

Jack Freeman, wholesale beef distributor and longtime P.S. resident, used to lose there, when he couldn't get up to Vegas. "I easily lost a million dollars in my time," he remembers. Frank Bogert remembers all-night gambling sessions with Charlie Farrell and the Hollywood stars who frequented his Racquet Club. All the old-timers in Palm Springs remember the Dunes, usually with a faint chuckle and a sigh for wilder times. On a good evening, you might run into Marlene Dietrich, Darryl Zanuck, Robert Montgomery, Clark Gable, Carole Lombard, the Ritz Brothers, or Errol Flynn over the craps and roulette games.

The Dunes was a class act. It was built by the notorious Al Wertheimer, a member of Detroit's Purple Gang, who sashayed into town in 1934 at the height of Palm Springs' booming reputation as Playground to the Stars. The stars, indeed, had more money than anyone else in the Depression, and gambling was the favored evening entertainment. So what if it was against the law? In Palm Springs, nobody cared. Wertheimer paid off the local cop, Sheriff Rayburn, who vanished completely just after the casino burned down.

Wertheimer had the nerve to attempt a club in Palm Springs itself, but he was hounded out of town by local church groups and the indefatigable Nellie Coffman, owner of the Desert Inn. Undaunted as a man with high connections can be, Al built his Spanish-style stucco palace in the middle of a sand-blown field, outfitted it with a gun-toting watchman and heavily armed maître d', a real French chef and black-tie waiters, "high tablecloth" service, chandeliers, gilt-edged china, fine-cut crystal. Nothing in Beverly Hills or New York was grander than the Dunes in trashy old Cathedral City, but like the Racquet Club it was an exclusive spot. You had to be known to the management to get in, or come as a guest of some established customer—and in particular Wertheimer refused to admit local yokels who lacked connections to the celebrity tourists and high rollers. He was wise enough to avoid the charge of corrupting poor working folks or taking food from their children's mouths.

The Dunes, you see, in addition to being outside the law, was also rigged, crooked, unfairly advantageous to the house. Everyone seems to admit that now, but in the flush years they either didn't know or didn't care. You could win a lot of money at the Dunes, but you were more likely to lose a lot. Wertheimer employed an aide, George the Greek, whose specialty was switching to loaded dice when a player had a chance to win big.

Wertheimer was certainly generous to local schools, youth groups, and charities. And he pretty much operated in the open. The big hotels, like El Mirador and the Racquet Club, offered phone lines to the Dunes so guests could place their bets on horse races at Santa Anita or Aqueduct. Casino money directly and indirectly contributed to the founding of the Desert Circus, a big parade and town celebration that raised funds for good causes and built Our Lady of Solitude Church opposite Liberace's house on Alejo Road. It's fair to say that the illicit gambling enterprise made Palm Springs what it became, because without the lure of the crap tables and the finest orchestras and entertainment, the movie stars would not have found the desert as appealing as they did.

Big Al came to a bad end, of course, as did the Dunes. Wertheimer had the misfortune, like Teddy Kennedy, to be behind the wheel of a car with a woman—Beatrice Manni—who wasn't his wife and moreover was married to an MGM studio executive. She died in the accident they had, he was gravely injured, and shortly thereafter, in 1943, the club burned down to the ground in an arson fire. Nobody bothered to look for suspects or to rebuild the property.

Al came back over the town line into Palm Springs and opened a restaurant, also called the Dunes, on Palm Canyon Drive. Eventually

▲ Pie-eyed Dean Martin (R) leads some table talk at Ray Ryan's (L) club. (Photo courtesy Paul Pospesil Collection)

he sold it to pal Irwin Rubenstein, who rechristened it Ruby's Dunes. This one dining spot has been the scene of countless disturbances of the peace ever since, including one incarnation as Gatsby's, another as Winners Sports Bar, headquarters for riotous Spring Break misadventures, and a current existence as Confetti. Palm Springs, in its infinite affection for sleaze, has erected a plaque in front of the bar commemorating it as the "historical" site of Ruby's Dunes—where Frank Sinatra had to be helped off his knees after nights of heavy drinking, where college kids now bounce out to barf in the gutter.

In 1948, Wertheimer attempted another gambling operation, this time out of his private home and intimate hotel, the Colonial House in Palm Springs, but he was busted and handed a sixty-day sentence. He died in 1953, broke and in disgrace.

Another casino that lacked the class of the Dunes, but was easier to get into, was the 139 Club, also in Cathedral City. Operated by heaving-drinking Earl Sausser, the 139 was no class joint with Continental cuisine and candelabras like the Dunes. It had sawdust on the floors, served free chili, and attracted a broader clientele ranging from Hollywood celebrities to ordinary working stiffs. It had an actual stone turret with a gunman posted inside, but the atmosphere was friendly, until things turned dangerous.

Earl Sausser died in 1942, leaving operation of the 139 to his lawyer, Walter Melrose, who managed to keep it running until 1947 despite increasing heat from the feds. Meanwhile a third casino, the Cove, had opened in Cathedral City, and it took over some of the exclusive former clientele of the Dunes. Run by Frank Portnoy, an associate of Wertheimer's, and Jake Katelman, who made his fortune building parking lots in L.A., the Cove aspired to some of the elegance of the original Dunes, but it came along too late. Even with protection provided by Sheriff Rayburn, the club was constantly forced to close down because of FBI pressures. Katelman and Portnoy gave up and moved to Las Vegas, where they could operate legally without the hassles of a new Palm Springs intent on cleaning up its act.

The 139 Club became a thrift shop for the Humane Society before it was torn down in 1985. The Cove was sold to the Elks. The only legal gambling in the desert now is on the Indian reservations, but not because current Cathedral City mayor George Hardie hasn't been trying his best to return casino gambling to his much-maligned town.

Cathedral City, despite its pretty name and the distinction of being the fastest-growing town in California in the 1980's, has always been Palm Springs' dumping grounds. It now has the only pornographic book and video stores in the desert, most of the gay night spots, and some of the trashiest bars, and it is preparing to institute an "adult zone."

Palm Springs Life

California's Prestige Magazine

AUGUST 1988/$3.75

The Green-Felt Desert?

Casino-Style Gambling:
Rumor or Reality?

A Look at Palm Springs'
Gambling Times

Plus:
Las Vegas & Laughlin

What's New New York City:
Top Designers Preview
Fall Fashion

And Much More!

And mayor Hardie just happens to be the general manager and a minority share owner of the Bicycle Club in Bell Gardens (Los Angeles county), a legal card game parlor which in March 1990 was seized by the federal government amid allegations that it was built with laundered drug money. Hardie denies any knowledge of these funds, and his investor group's 35 percent of the casino was released by the government.

The Bicycle Club, the largest card casino in the world, was the single greatest asset ever seized by the U.S. Government. Its original investors put up a total of only $10,000 yet realized an incredible $50 million profit between 1985 and 1990. The government contends that $12 million in drug profits was channeled through foreign banks by the late Sam Gilbert, a noted Los Angeles developer, and used to build the casino, now valued at $150 million.

Meanwhile, George Hardie fought long and hard to bring a similar casino operation to Cathedral City in 1989, but his pro-gambling proposition was soundly defeated at the polls. George Hardie has spent a lifetime pushing gambling onto reluctant California communities, however, and he hasn't given up.

Many desert residents believe that the new Palm Springs Convention Center and glittering hotels built in the eighties are "wired for gambling," set up with the technical capacity to convert overnight into major league casino operations. Allegations to that effect have appeared in print. Some fervently want a kind of Vegas in P.S., believing that would be the only way to revive the local economy, while others just as passionately oppose the development. Mayor Sonny Bono denies absolutely that the Convention Center is wired, but nobody takes him seriously. How would he know, anyway?

◀ *Palm Springs Life* featured historical coverage of the old casinos in the August 1988 issue. Nobody is in P.S. in August if they can help it, and that issue is always the slimmest of the year. (Photo courtesy *Palm Springs Life*)

Ric-Su-Dar

The Zanucks in Palm Springs

Darryl F. Zanuck, the profligate head honcho of Twentieth Century Fox, left a trail of hushed gossip about his estate in Palm Springs, Ric-Su-Dar, and its wild society. One of Zanuck's grandsons, Raymond "Dino" Hakim, even tried to turn the place into a brothel to raise money for his dope habit. The great mogul brought his Parisian mistress there under his wife's nose and wound up retiring in Palm Springs after his fall from grace.

Zanuck bought the fabulous estate from producer Joseph Schenck in 1943, renaming it Ric-Su-Dar in honor of his three children, Richard, Susan, and Darrylin. All three would grow disenchanted with their father, who chased around the world with a succession of girlfriends (including actresses Bella Darvi and Juliette Greco, both DFZ "discoveries"), dissipating the resources of the studio, while his wife Virginia held the home front and joined a stockholders' revolt against him.

It was (and is) a sprawling complex with a two-story main house, plus a pool house with four bedrooms, a piay area called the casino, a

70-foot-long swimming pool, and tennis courts. The jolly group that gathered there called it the "Palm Springs Yacht Club." They included regulars Joseph Cotten, Douglas Fairbanks, Jr., David Niven, Jennifer Jones, David Selznick, Tyrone Power, Clifton Webb, Judy Garland, Noel Coward, and Rita Hayworth carrying a baby she thought was Aly Khan's but staying with other guys. The main sport played was lawn croquet, with much shouting and mayhem—although musical beds was another popular game, with guests tiptoeing from one bedroom to another through the night.

In the glory years of the forties and early fifties, when Darryl and Virginia were still together and hosting parties, and Fox was booming, Ric-Su-Dar saw glittering banquets and drunken brawls, a constant party of whirlwind proportions. Virginia was the unflappable hostess, blasé even in the face of smashed chandeliers and guests falling into the pool. A favorite parlor game was "Murder," with the guest holding the ace of spades as "murderer" and another person as "victim." Some of these games got too real to be funny.

When Zanuck left the family, Virginia retained Ric-Su-Dar in addition to homes in Hollywood and elsewhere, as a kind of original family home. She never divorced her husband, insisted on being addressed as "Mrs. Darryl F. Zanuck," and perhaps thought the house would someday lure him back. She didn't live there, however, except for occasional visits. Darryl stayed there for a time in 1967 with his French mistress, Genevieve Gillaizeau, who performed under the name Genevieve Gilles. She was by all accounts without talent, except the ability to charm DFZ. Her career was a disaster, costly to the studio and embarrassing to Zanuck's reputation as a star builder.

Genevieve accompanied Zanuck when he returned to Palm Springs in April 1973 for a reconciliation with his wife and a final, fatal move into Ric-Su-Dar. By then, he had been ousted from control of Fox and had descended into a kind of senility we would now call Alzheimer's disease, in which he gradually lost touch with reality and the world. "Where are Darryl and I supposed to sleep?" Gilles demanded when they entered the complex—but she was enraged to learn that she was to have no further access to her lover.

More than ten lawsuits were filed against Zanuck's estate, some

▲ Ric-Su-Dar, Darryl F. Zanuck's fabulous 1.5 acre estate in the heart of Palm Springs, is obscured and protected behind thick walls. Sold for $1.2 million in 1990 to Ann Eisenhower, Ike's niece, it is used for lavish parties. (Photo courtesy of the author)

of them still pending. More suits were filed against Virginia's estate after she left everything to Darrylin and stiffed Richard and his children with $5,000 each.

RIC: Richard Zanuck was the oldest child and only son, and he followed in his father's footsteps so well that his production successes (including *Jaws* and *The Sting*) eventually overshadowed DFZ's most colossal hits. But not before father and son had come to bitter enmity. In the failed palace coup of December, 1970, Darryl orchestrated the firing of Richard from his position at Fox after Richard had attempted to be named president, the object being to ease the old man into a chairmanship of the board role.

But DFZ felt threatened, and the son found himself locked out, barred from the studio lot where he'd virtually grown up, summarily ejected from the premises without a day's notice. He left his office and walked to his car only to find a hired studio hand painting his name out of the vehicle door.

Darryl and Richard were never friends again, although the son did return to Ric-Su-Dar to see his father reinstalled in Palm Springs.

SU: Susan Zanuck died of massive alcohol consumption in Palm Springs on June 10, 1980, at the age of forty-six, just six months after DFZ breathed his last at Desert Hospital (December 22, 1979). Unlike her brother, she never worked in the film industry but lived off the family fortune and maintained a lifestyle of complete dissipation. Drunk from morning to night, she kept a filthy household and was incapable of taking care of her children, who were variously taken away by their father or watched over by grandmother Virginia at Ric-Su-Dar. The family more than once paid off the Palm Springs police to get Susan out of trouble and keep her embarrassing escapades out of the press.

One of Susan's kids, Raymond "Dino" Hakim, was also in trouble from the first. Gay, drug-addicted, and actively involved in dealing drugs, he was threatened by dealers to whom he owed money. Taken from Susan in 1975, he was originally showered with gifts at Ric-Su-Dar, but was later thrown out for trying to turn the upstairs bedrooms into a whorehouse to raise money for his habit. Dino died at age twenty-two on April 26, 1981, of choking on his own vomit after an overdose of morphine and cocaine. He was buried with his favorite cassette tapes, headphones, and drug paraphernalia.

DAR: Darrylin, the remaining daughter, came into her mother's favor and inherited by far the greatest share of the family's fortune, although embroiled in bitter litigation.

The Ric-Su-Dar complex went on the market for sale in 1988 and was finally sold in late 1990. It's in the older part of Palm Springs that was once glamorous but is now seedy and run-down. While the money went "down valley" to Indian Wells, Palm Desert, and such, Ric-Su-Dar went downhill to a sad condition of neglect, its swimming pool empty and stained, gang graffiti on its walls, and prostitutes working its block. If those empty rooms could talk, what tales they'd tell of a life gone haywire in the desert.

Going His Way

Der Bingle in the Desert

THERE IS A FAMOUS photograph of Bing Crosby, obviously drunk, toasting the New Year of 1940 with a silly hat on his head, taken at the El Mirador's annual champagne blast. Crosby was a heavy drinker during his first marriage to Dixie Lee, who was born Wilma Winifred Wyatt on November 4, 1911, and died November 1, 1952, of cancer, booze, and some say, Bing's abuse. He was sentenced to thirty days in jail for illegal alcohol possession during Prohibition, but he did curtail his intake in his later years.

Crosby managed to fabricate for himself a media image of the perfect loving father, husband, sweet guy crooner, the man everybody loved. Half the nation believed he was really Father Flanagan, rehearsing the street boys in "Swinging on a Star." In fact, it's now well documented that he was self-centered, brutally abusive to his children, cold to his friends, and indifferent to his wife's illness. As she lay dying in 1952, he went to France to make a picture.

Rudy Vallee worked with Bing on the Fleischmann Hour on early radio, and said, "There was ice water in all the Crosby veins, but especially in Bing's." Vallee and Crosby were also singing rivals at the Racquet Club in the thirties. Rudy loved to get up and entertain the Hollywood set with his songs, and by all accounts it was near impossible to make him sit down.

◄ Bing Crosby with first wife Dixie Lee and their children, from left, Phillip, Lindsay, Gary, and Dennis. (Star File)

76

▲ Bing Crosby was by all accounts far from the nicest guy in Palm Springs. (Photo courtesy Paul Pospesil Collection)

▲ Der Bingle eyeing a young lady's dress. (Photo courtesy Paul Pospesil Collection)

Crosby developed an act of pretending to be the bartender while he was delivering a song. The actual bartender, Tex Gregg, would hand Bing a fresh bottle of Glenlivet Scotch, which Crosby poured into the guests' glasses as he circled the room. Those who were already drinking Scotch were delighted. The others had to suffer Scotch mixed with their vodka or gin or bourbon, which meant either tossing the drink out or tossing it down their throats at the risk of a killer Palm Springs hangover.

Bing had more than his share of women in Palm Springs, even while Dixie Lee was still alive. Son Gary, at the age of seventeen, had walked in on dear old Dad and one of his overnight playmates. Grace Kelly was among the conquests.

Actress Kathryn Grant (Olive Kathryn Grandstaff) visited Bing in P.S. in October, 1954, and he proposed marriage in the desert later that year. With Kathryn, Bing had a second family and gravitated away from Palm Springs toward northern California, where they built their estate in Hillsborough and moved his prestigious golf tournament to Pebble Beach.

Phil Harris, Bing's great fishing partner and desert buddy, remained in Palm Springs and married Alice Faye, and now manages Frank Sinatra's annual February golf tournament when he is not hanging out in the city's watering holes swinging deals, currying favor, and telling jokes. He went from the payroll of the Crooner to be spokesperson for the Man.

▼ Bing cuts the rug with his second wife, Kathryn, who was twenty-three at the time he proposed to her in Palm Springs. The crooner was fifty-five himself. (Photo courtesy Frank Bogert Collection)

Desert
Desilu
Follies

LUCILLE BALL AND DESI ARNAZ were on the scene in Palm Springs by the early 1950s, being photographed taking tennis lessons at the Racquet Club, carousing at the Doll House restaurant owned by George and Ethel Strebe ("my family keeps bugging me to write down the history of what happened at the Doll House," said George, now in his eighties, "but I'm still thinking about it"), finally building one of the first fairway homes at the exclusive Thunderbird Country Club in Rancho Mirage, managed by (who else?) Frank Bogert, after he ran the El Mirador and the Racquet Club.

(The Thunderbird became so famous and synonymous with wealth and power that it is much imitated in Palm Springs. There are a dozen listings in the phone book for resorts and businesses called "Thunderbird" something, most of them unrelated to the country club—including Thunderbird Security, Thunderbird Terrace Security, and Thunderbird Property Owners Security. The security surrounding the golf course is armed.)

Lucy and Desi became royal figures in the desert, on a par with Bing Crosby, Frank Sinatra, and Bob Hope, and Desi is credited with having been one of the first to colonize Indian Wells. He was the honorary mayor and was on the ground floor in building the posh Indian

◄ Lucy and Desi arrive by helicopter, headed no doubt for the soon-to-be New Lost World. (Photo courtesy Paul Pospesil Collection)

82

▲ Lucy and Desi step out in the desert. Desi was seldom seen without a bodyguard. (Photo courtesy Paul Pospesil Collection)

Wells Country Club, which in 1990 was sold to the Japanese, who think nothing of charging a million dollars for a golf membership.

Lucy was fairly demure, protecting her image as the all American housewife and mother of "Little Ricky," but Desi blazed a path of hard drinking, hard bargaining, and all-night gambling and womanizing with the best of them. Frank Sinatra once threatened to kill him because he

▲ Frank Bogert with Lucy, who dyed her hair red in Palm Springs. (Photo courtesy Paul Pospesil Collection)

thought Desilu Productions' hit TV show, "The Untouchables," was a slur on the Mafia and Italians in general. Sinatra and Arnaz faced off in a boozy confrontation at the Indian Wells Country Club, but Desi's two bodyguards were bigger and meaner than Frank's two bodyguards, and he laughed off the singer's menacing words.

The pattern of Desilu desert folly started in Palm Springs and branched ever eastward through Rancho Mirage and Indian Wells. Before the Thunderbird was built, the couple had a private estate near Bob Hope Drive, just a little walled kingdom with bungalows for 75 couples, a dozen tennis courts, stables with horses, and ample room in the canyons for riding. Eventually, in 1982, this sprawling complex was turned into probably the most lavish resort for gays and lesbians in the world. They called it the New Lost World, and I was lost there for a week once myself.

We flew into Palm Springs and were met at the airport by an impossibly good-looking blond young fellow in a bright green New Lost World polo shirt and crisp white shorts, who drove us out to Rancho Mirage and checked us into the resort. Then it was nonstop drinking and doping and sexual titillation behind the safely guarded security barriers. The New Lost World featured three swimming pools (one specified for nudes), two restaurants, a four-star French place for formal dining, and a coffee shop for relaxed snacking, plus two bars and a nightly male burlesque striptease show.

As is still the pattern in many small, private resorts in Palm Springs today, the New Lost World offered its guests access to walk-in private larders heavily stocked with every imaginable kind of food, booze, and personal hygiene item, sold at the same price the owners had paid at the supermarket. You simply picked up whatever groceries and liquor you wanted, signed for them on the honor system, and took them back to your room. In effect, you never had to leave the New Lost World for anything you needed. Once checked in, you could walk around bare-ass, borrow free X-rated videotapes from the front desk, drink and fuck with abandon.

But the New Lost World is no more, alas—another Palm Springs business failure. The gates to the place are firmly padlocked, with hostile "keep out" signs posted alongside the "for sale by sheriff's auction" announcements.

Lucy and Desi went on to better things. She became America's most revered comedienne, while he slipped out of the public eye and out of town. Desi passed away in 1986. Lucy continued to live in the desert part-time until her death in 1989. Desi Arnaz, Jr., virtually born on TV on January 19, 1953, left the desert for the coastal resort of Ojai, near Santa Barbara.

Hope Springs
Infernal

OB HOPE AND HIS WIFE Dolores have both been named honorary mayor of Palm Springs, and both are tied to the city's history and current development, identified in the public mind as Palm Springs royalty. There's even a major street named Bob Hope Drive, spanning from Interstate 10 to Highway 111, crossing Frank Sinatra, Fred Waring, Dinah Shore, and Gerald Ford drives through Rancho Mirage to Palm Desert. But when Hope's house burned down in 1973, he couldn't get help from the Palm Springs Fire Department "because they have an unlisted phone number," he joked.

The comedian lives in Toluca Lake, but you can see his house from the main highway in Palm Springs, set on a hillside with a pool in the shape of the familiar Hope profile.

Hope has spent most of his career developing the goody-gumdrops image of a patriotic and charitable do-gooder, but he has managed to amass one of the biggest personal fortunes in the world, and he's not known for sharing it or giving it away.

He didn't get limitlessly rich on his talent, either, since he doesn't particularly sing, dance, or act, and his jokes are funny only to people over seventy-five. (Hope was born May 29, 1903, in Eltham, England.) He's never won an Oscar. He got rich by investing in real estate in Palm Springs and Los Angeles decades before anyone else saw the potential. Bob Hope wound up owning some huge parcels of the choicest land in the Southland—including what is now Eisenhower Medical Center in

◄ Bob gets one of his many medals. (Photo courtesy Paul Pospesil Collection)

88

Rancho Mirage and vast stretches of the ecologically priceless Santa Monica Mountains.

In 1990, although under fire from environmental nonprofit groups trying to preserve what is left of the mountain wilderness in southern California, Hope refused to sell his Jordan Ranch property to the National Park Service and instead offered a deal that could set the worst precedent in its history. Hope wants to sell Jordan Ranch to developers for luxury homes and a golf course, but the only access to his land is across National Park land.

In exchange for the easement which will allow him to destroy 60 acres of pristine wilderness with his subdivision, Hope offered to donate 800 acres of rocky, undevelopable goat country at three nearby sites to the Park Service and state parks. He then tried to portray this as an act of great generosity and public-spiritedness.

The hard-core Hope fans were no doubt taken in, but not everyone was fooled. *Los Angeles Times* columnist Robert A. Jones called it "a deal from the heart of darkness. A deal that leaves blood on everybody's hands, most notably those trying to save the Santa Monicas. A deal so Faustian that it makes you want to look away. An evil deal.

"Let Hope have his golf course and his subdivisions and give us our squares of the checkerboard. Maybe later we can wash the blood of Jordan Ranch and Corral Canyon from our hands. But if this deal goes through, please spare us the 'Thank you, Mr. Hope' business. We paid for this one, and we paid pretty big," Jones wrote.

Reader Rosie McCabe of Agoura added: "The purpose of this exchange is for a massive, up-zoned development in Jordan Ranch. The proposed PGA golf course will be 'plopped' on one of the last oak forests in southern California. Without parkland access, the developer could not put 1,152 homes and the golf course where 14 ranches are currently allowed. . . . Let's not call this business exchange a donation!"

No less a person than Walter Annenberg jumped to Hope's defense, writing in the letters column of the *Los Angeles Times* that "what has saddened me is the recent display of letters vilifying this patriot, largely because he has participated in successful real estate investments. . . . The frequent discouragement philanthropists learn is that no good deed may go unpunished."

The only major presence Hope still maintains in Palm Springs is

▲ Bob Hope's famous house can be seen from the main highway in town, complete with a swimming pool in his profile. (Photo courtesy Frank Bogert Collection)

his annual golf tournament, started in 1964 as the Bob Hope Classic in an attempt to rival Bing Crosby's more successful Pebble Beach tournament, "the Crosby." Now called the Bob Hope Chrysler Classic, the event was heavily criticized in 1990 under the new PGA Tour antidiscrimination rules because two golf courses hosting it—the Bermuda Dunes Country Club and La Quinta Country Club—have absolutely no black members. La Quinta general manager Robert Moore has gone on record as saying that his golf course never had a black person apply for membership.

You wouldn't apply if you were black, either. It's well known that blacks were unwelcome in Palm Springs in the old days, so much so

▲ Casa Hope burns to the ground July 24, 1973. Temperature in Palm Springs was 108 degrees. (Photo courtesy Frank Bogert Collection)

that the town of Val Verde, forty miles northwest of Los Angeles, sprang up in the 1930s "as a kind of black Palm Springs," according to black realtor Dalton Celaius, a sixteen-year resident. Count Basie and Duke Ellington gave open-air concerts there after being snubbed by Palm Springs.

Hope may not be personally responsible for the racist policies of his golf course hosts, but he was entirely silent in the face of PGA charges.

▶ Bob and Dolores were each honorary Mayor of Palm Springs at different times. (Photo courtesy Paul Pospesil Collection)

Ring-a-
Ding-Ding

Hooray for the King

I<small>N THIS TOWN</small>," said Shirley MacLaine to Frank Sinatra in Palm Springs, "you're a closet dictator."

Not so much in the closet. In the public view, Ol' Blue Eyes was "Mr. Palm Springs" just as Charlie Farrell was before him and Sonny Bono is now. And despite much drunkenness and bad public behavior, Sinatra was never disciplined or even criticized, rather lionized into a hero and a wide boulevard. Now, in his old age, he's a major patron of Desert Hospital and Eisenhower Medical Center through his annual golf tournament and gala dinners, at which the Man can be counted on to sing if he's able to stand.

His aggressive tantrums and omnipresent bodyguards are legends in Palm Springs, where beefy sidekick "Jerry the Crusher" got his charming nickname from crushing Coca Cola bottles with his bare hands and spreading the pieces around the grounds of Sinatra's Tamarisk Country Club home, where he lived with Ava Gardner for a time after his first marriage to Nancy Barbato broke up.

Frank met Ava in the Chi Chi Club in Palm Springs in 1950. He was dancing with Lana Turner, and Howard Hughes was dancing with Ava. When the bandleader said, "Change partners," Frank and Ava ended up dancing off together and roaring away in his car.

◄ Sinatra and P.S. police officer enjoy the company of a desert lounge lady. (Photo courtesy Paul Pospesil Collection)

► Bombshell Ava Gardner kept the keys to Sinatra's Palm Springs home long after their divorce, though the relationship was strictly platonic by then. (Photo courtesy Star File)

Their relationship was to be a stormy one, however—so violent that even the Palm Springs police got called in. They married in November, 1951, but on October 21, 1952, Frank called the cops and threw both Ava and Lana into the street for allegedly talking about him behind his back, comparing his sexual prowess (unfavorably) to that of bandleader Artie Shaw. (This despite the fact that Ava, when asked by an interviewer what she saw in "that 120 pound shrimp, Sinatra," replied, "Frank is only 10 pounds, the other 110 pounds are all cock.") After loudly evicting the girls, Sinatra himself spent the night at songwriter Jimmy Van Heusen's house, throwing up. Both Ava and Lana were also married to Shaw, whom Frank tried to warn away from Ava, without success.

For all the bad times, Ava remained a true friend to Frank even beyond their marriage, which broke up with an official MGM divorce announcement October 29, 1953. Long after he married Barbara Marx and she was seeing other men, they spoke on the phone frequently. "People who say nasty things about him are full of dirt," Ava said in 1975. "He's maligned by the press worse than anybody else. They don't know him. They don't bother to find out who he is, what he is, all the wonderful things that he does."

Not that Sinatra has made himself all that available to the press. In 1959, he posted a sign outside his Palm Springs house: "If you haven't been invited, you better have a damn good reason for ringing this bell!" At his current address, 70588 Frank Sinatra Drive, in Rancho Mirage, conditions are no more welcoming. The sign reads, "Forget the dog. Beware of the owner." And all of this befits a man who has been associated with such notorious Mafia kingpins as Sam Giancana (whose mistress, Judith Campbell, also slept with President John F. Kennedy through Frank's introduction), John Rosselli, Carlos Marcello, and Anthony Accardo.

It was precisely Sinatra's association with organized crime, and Palm Springs' reputation as a friendly hideout for Mafia honchos, that led Robert Kennedy as Attorney General of the U.S. to persuade his brother Jack to stay at Republican crooner Bing Crosby's house rather than Sinatra's place when the President visited town March 24 to 26, 1962.

▶ Lana Turner affects a schoolmarm posture. She was with Ava Gardner the night Sinatra threw her out. (Photo courtesy Paul Pospesil Collection)

Sinatra had worked long and hard on Kennedy's 1960 campaign, had visited JFK in the family compound at Hyannisport, and had staged a lavish gala as part of the president's inauguration. He also provided JFK with Hollywood starlets and models for his insatiable sexual appetite. So it seemed to Frank only natural that his Palm Springs home would become a kind of Western White House; and with no apparent authorization from anyone, Sinatra broke ground a month after the election on a lavish Presidential guest house with accommodations for JFK, his family, the Secret Service, and forty guests, plus a helicopter

▼ Barbara Sinatra and Ernest Noya, president of the Palm Springs Senior Center. (Photo courtesy Paul Pospesil Collection)

▲ Sinatra tools with sauces. Note the jumbo cocktail by the pot. (Photo courtesy Paul Pospesil Collection)

pad, a sophisticated phone bank, extra security—even a flagpole mimicking the one at Hyannisport, where Old Glory was to be flown to indicate when the president was in residence.

But Bobby would have none of it, and so JFK stayed at Bing's place instead—where he was joined by Marilyn Monroe on March 24, 1962. The official reason was that Crosby had better security, but that didn't assuage Frank's rage, which he vented at Peter Lawford, JFK's

▲ A young Frank with prize grapefruit and best bud Jimmy Van Heusen, who tolerated the crooner's tantrums. (Photo courtesy Paul Pospesil Collection)

actor brother-in-law, to whom fell the dreaded fate of breaking the news to Sinatra. Sinatra didn't speak to Lawford again for many years. (It wasn't the first time he quarreled with Peter, but it was the last. On New Year's Eve, 1958, Sinatra bolted to Palm Springs after a drunken argument with Lawford at a Hollywood party. Peter and his wife Patricia kept some clothing at Frank's house in Palm Springs, which Sinatra set on fire and threw into his swimming pool.)

▼ Lauren Bacall, Frank, and songwriter Jimmy Van Heusen share an intense moment. Frank went to Jimmy's house to throw up after tossing Ava Gardner into the street. (Photo courtesy Paul Pospesil Collection)

▲ Mia Farrow consorted with and married Sinatra, but dated John Phillips while they were married.

Kennedy's snub in favor of Crosby—a Republican no less—further deteriorated Sinatra's standing with Mafia boss Giancana, whom Frank had led to believe that he was capable of "delivering" Kennedy's favors. And in 1963, the Nevada State Gaming Commission forced Sinatra to give up his nine percent interest in the Sands casino in Las Vegas because of his continuing association with Giancana.

Sinatra married Mia Farrow on July 19, 1966, when he was fifty and she was twenty-two. Ava Gardner reportedly quipped, "I always knew Frank would end up in bed with a boy." They met while Frank was acting in *Von Ryan's Express* and Mia in TV's *Peyton Place,* and soon they were flying to Palm Springs every weekend in Frank's private jet. They became the hottest couple in the hot town, and maybe the world.

Farrow showed up black and blue on the set of *Johnny Belinda*. And by two years into their marriage, in 1968, when Mia had finished making *Rosemary's Baby* and was estranged from Sinatra although still married to him, she and John Phillips of the Mamas and the Papas singing group began seeing a lot of each other. Phillips used to pick Mia up at Frank's desert compound and drive her to the Joshua Tree Inn in the high desert.

Frank was livid once the scandal sheets got hold of the story. But there wasn't much he could do about it. The marriage lasted only two years.

No more a loyal Democrat, Frank eventually transformed his wanna-be-JFK-presidential guest home into the so-called Agnew House for Vice President Spiro T. Agnew during the Nixon administration. Agnew stayed on in the desert and now lives in Rancho Mirage not too far from Annenberg's fortress. Sinatra found the kind of social acceptance and public honor from Nixon and the Republicans that Kennedy had denied him. In 1985, Ronald Reagan awarded him the Presidential Medal of Freedom.

Frank married Barbara Marx at Annenberg's estate in 1976, and they are still together. Barbara became a Marx by marrying Zeppo Marx, of the Marx Brothers, who was considerably older than she was and reportedly dependent on Groucho for regular support checks. But he gave her an entrée into membership in the Racquet Club and association with high-ranking Palm Springs society.

▲ Leonore Annenberg. Frank and Barbara seem etched in stone at the Sinatra Sculpture Court, one of their desert charities. (Photo courtesy Paul Pospesil Collection)

◄ Barbara Marx Sinatra, a Las Vegas showgirl made good in Palm Springs. (Photo courtesy Paul Pospesil Collection)

▲ Frank's an untouchable in Palm Springs society. (Photo courtesy Paul Pospesil Collection)

And Barbara was seeing Frank even while still married to poor old Zeppo. Her nocturnal comings and goings and way of slipping out in the morning reportedly offended Agnew's wife, Judy. But nobody told Zeppo and nobody confronted Frank.

Today, Frank has his picture on the cover of *Palm Springs Life* magazine every February issue—without exception—to coincide with his annual golf and social get-together to benefit Desert Hospital. (Bob

◄ Barbara seems pleased with a portrait of herself. (Photo courtesy Paul Pospesil Collection)

Hope is on every January cover, Dinah Shore every March, and so forth. *Palm Springs Life* doesn't mind being called predictable, as long as the formula makes money.) The Children's Center at Eisenhower Medical Center was named after Barbara Sinatra. Together, these two pose as benign royalty of the desert swamp—a pair of show-biz types made respectable by bottomless money. At seventy-five, the Voice can't really sing any more although the faithful continue to attend his boozy attempts at concert making. His July 10, 1990, concert at Glasgow,

▲ Ol' Blue Eyes flanked by guards. (Photo courtesy Paul Pospesil Collection)

Scotland, was such an embarrassment that Sinatra had to concede to a "very significant" cut in his fees, and seating was repositioned so that the original thirty thousand tickets were reduced to eleven thousand. Even then, seats went empty and begging.

But Palm Springs loves its closet dictator, and always will.

Do You Know the Way to the Way to Danny Kaye?

Palm Springs Streets Named after Celebrities

Andrews Circle (Andrews Sisters)

Walter Annenberg Drive

Arthur Ashe Lane

Gene Autry Trail

Ralph Bellamy Road

Jack Benny Road

Burns & Allen Road

Claudette Colbert Road

Bing Crosby Drive

Charles Farrell Drive

Gerald Ford Drive

Greer Garson Road

Bob Hope Drive

Danny Kaye Road

Groucho Marx Road

Jack Nicklaus Road

Arnold Palmer Road

Dinah Shore Drive

Frank Sinatra Drive

Barbara Stanwyck Road

Fred Waring Drive

Normandy
Remembered

Is Errol Flynn Turning Over
in His Grave?

WHEN THE CASA DEL SOL Hotel on Indian Avenue burned down in August, 1990—yet another unsolved arson fire in Palm Springs and only a block from Desert Hospital (the former El Mirador hotel), where the historic tower was torched a year earlier—James Alderson of North Palm Springs remembered the days when Errol Flynn presided over the wild parties at poolside.

Flynn built the Casa del Sol in 1943, calling it the Normandy. "Such a beautiful place it was," recalled Alderson, who was manager of the hotel and lived there for five years. "It was built for himself and his friends as a retreat from the hectic ways of Hollywood. In the forties and fifties, there were nothing but movie stars laying in the sun around the pool. It had four suites, nine double and nine single rooms. But Flynn's personal suite was really something, with an enormous fireplace, huge bedroom, two baths—one with a tub and one with a shower—and a very large living room."

The two giant palm trees in front of Flynn's suite were imported to Palm Springs from the Caribbean by the actor himself. It was nonstop party time at the Normandy. "A good time was had by all," Alderson reminisced. "It had to be the best time in my life."

◄ Who, me? Errol Flynn was a dashing presence at poolside, especially where bronzed young men were lounging. (Photo courtesy Star File)

The Casa del Sol is now a burned-out disaster, charred timbers still standing around what was once a lavish pool setting. The hotel next to it, so close by it's almost touching, suddenly sprouted a "for sale" sign. Called the Silver Sands, formerly Michael's Inn, the building for sale is owned by Don Meharry of Meharry Development Corp., a gay entrepreneur. Meharry's longtime companion Dennis died in January, 1990. His other hotel, the Hideaway in Rancho Mirage, is closed down except for private parties.

Errol Flynn might have appreciated the irony of his Normany Hotel winding up next door to a notorious gay-oriented spot. Flynn was reportedly bisexual at least. And Michael's Inn/Silver Sands was noted for its clothing-optional policy and its boutique featuring men's underwear, swimsuits, amyl nitrate poppers, and anal lubricants.

What Will the
Old Ladies
Think?

When he came here, he was more or less a loner—but friendly with everyone," said Allen Keller, current reigning Queen of Palm Springs ("and the only man in town who's had a mastectomy"), of Liberace. The flamboyant entertainer died in his P. S. mansion, Casa de las Cloisters, of AIDS-related symptoms on February 4, 1987, but not before he blazed new trails of decadence and self-indulgence in the sizzling village.

He arrived in 1952, the same year his television show made its debut, and bought several smaller houses before purchasing the Cloisters, including the Safari Room, with imitation animal-skin wallpaper, the Valentino Suite highlighted by a brass sleigh-bed and chandelier that once belonged to Rudolph Valentino (Liberace's middle name was Valentine), the Marie Antoinette Room filled with French antiques, and the Persian Tent Room for orgiastic fantasies.

And orgy he did. His master suite has a Jacuzzi the size of a swimming pool, a bathtub with mirrored walls and ceilings, and pornographic shower curtains. The house has four courtyards, one with an Olympic-sized pool. The lavish bar in the living room was designed so that guests could drive into the U-shaped driveway and be handed a cocktail the instant they walked through the door.

The house was opened for public viewing in April, 1990, just before the estate sold its contents at auction to benefit the Liberace Foundation, and before new owner Stefan Hemming, a wealthy friend of Liberace's from San Francisco, began renovating the dusty, dark, museum-like

◄ Liberace made a fetish of fur coats, hardly necessary in the Palm Springs heat. (Photo courtesy John Weston Collection)

▲ A young Liberace favored relatively tasteful clothing compared to his later extravagance. (Photo courtesy Paul Pospesil Collection)

complex. The stuff left in the Cloisters ranged from the sublime to the ridiculous, from the priceless to the truly tacky.

Included were a Louis XVI gilt-metal-mounted, sycamore-inlaid mahogany commode—one of many elegant toilets attesting to Liberace's concern for first-class potties—a large Sheffield plate Regency-styled mirror plateau; a German Baroque oak, elm, and ash cabinet; a Louis Phillipe rosewood piano; and a figural fountain in the shape of a naked boy embracing a swan. In the driveway, looking gorgeous if impractical, was a red boat-tailed speedster convertible in which Liberace used to arrive on stage, driven by his favorite chauffeur and bedmate, blond Scott Thorson. The car had a gas-tank capacity of one gallon and a

▲ Liberace with Al Anthony at the La Paz hotel in Palm Springs. (Photo courtesy Paul Pospesil Collection)

motor that looked like it might get five miles to a gallon. In the master bedroom, Liberace's bed was covered with a black diamond mink bedspread lined with silk and embroidered with the Liberace signature logo. Hanging in the closet was a full-length white mink coat.

So much for the good stuff. The house also included a mind-boggling assortment of pure, absolute, garage-sale-quality junk. Hideous sculpture and art, much of it plastic. Miniature pianos and automobiles, many sent to him by his fans. (Liberace was a pack rat, incapable of throwing anything out, even the worst crap.) A big stuffed male doll with erect penis. Cookie jars in various themes. Postcards and throw rugs and chipped china, of course many fake candelabras, a vinyl kitchen dining set too grody for the Goodwill store, a truly antique videocassette recorder that must have weighed 50 pounds, a cornucopia of kitschy collectibles reflecting the bad taste of an old queen. On his deathbed, Liberace said, "I don't want people to think I'm an old queen." He should have had a yard sale—in someone else's yard.

Someplace like Desert Hot Springs, where people who are too déclassé for Palm Springs are forced to go.

"The Cloisters, although less formal than Lee's other homes, was just as much a jumble of flash and trash," boyfriend Thorson wrote in his memoir, *Behind the Candelabra*. "A priceless bronze sat alongside furniture Lee found in Watts. Cement garden sculptures from Mexico stood next to authentic marbles from Italy. . . . Lee loved the clutter and waxed poetic as he told how he acquired each individual piece."

Liberace's mother Frances lived in her own studio behind the Cloisters, where she complained loudly about his steady parade of boyfriends and late night shenanigans. But, as mothers will, she fiercely denied her son's homosexuality—and so did he. At one point early in his career, Lee actually went to court to defend himself against the accusation of gayness—and he won the case. He had a pathological fear of offending his audience, which included a lot of old ladies madly in love with him. But he was seen everywhere in Palm Springs with his bevy of young lads. His accountant, Lucille Cunningham, told Thorson, "Lee's had a string of boys like you. . . . I've seen them come and go."

They came and went all up and down Palm Canyon Drive, in the famous Chi Chi Club (which James remembers Liberace once had the wild impulse to buy as a lark, as a place for him and his boys to frolic and "play for free"), in Ruby's Dunes, even in the produce aisles of the local supermarkets.

And his annual Christmas party at the Cloisters is something that Palm Springs has never seen again, and perhaps never will. All his stagehands and servants were invited, and all of them and their children received lavish gifts. Eighteen Christmas trees adorned the mansion, each dripping with ornaments. The ornaments alone cost $25,000 a year and had to be delivered by truckloads. The first Christmas of their five years together, he gave Scott "two diamond rings, a black mink coat, a white mink jacket, a coyote and leather coat, a sapphire cross, a gold watch wreathed in diamonds, lots of clothes, a Maltese puppy named Georgie, a schnauzer named Precious, and a basset named Lulu." (Liberace and Scott together had a total of twenty-six dogs, which Lee considered his "babies." With all the boys and dogs in his life, he was a veritable scoutmaster of the kinky.)

Erroll Flynn, Tyrone Power, and Clark Gable were among the macho he-man movie stars who hung around Palm Springs and may have shared some of Lee's boys. Power was a favorite guest of Darryl F. Zanuck's at his Ric-Su-Dar complex. Gable's bisexual liaisons in Palm Springs are the stuff of undocumented rumor.

Plastic surgery is the aspirin of Palm Springs—everybody takes it, sooner or later—and both Liberace and Scott Thorson underwent the knife, to make Lee look younger and Scott look more like Lee. Drugs were an important part of their life at the Cloisters, too. Lee favored prescription downers, painkillers, and mood pills; Scott got into heavy cocaine and freebasing.

Pornography became one of Liberace's chief obsessions, and he built a vast collection of gay videotapes, the kinkier the better, which he liked to watch in the company of visiting boys, including two French teenagers who became fixtures at the house and left Scott in a state of enraged jealousy. He knew that Liberace's personal favorite was three-way sex, with one boy on each end. He was a classic "chicken hawk," an older man who was sexually attracted to young teenage boys. Eventually, of course, Scott became too "old" in his twenties, and Lee lost interest.

While the French boys moved into the Cloisters, Scott moved out, hiding out in the entertainer's penthouse in L. A. until he was physically ejected by hired goons. Later, Scott filed a lawsuit, which dragged on from 1982 to 1986, ending when Lee paid him off in a settlement. Cary James, an eighteen-year-old chorus boy, replaced Scott as Liberace's main squeeze in Palm Springs, and was with him in the Cloisters when he died, ravaged by AIDS, on February 4, 1987.

The memorial service was held at Our Lady of Solitude Church on Alejo Street, just kitty-corner from the Cloisters. Despite his rampaging life, drugs, booze, boyfriends, sexual excesses, spreading of the AIDS virus, absolute indifference to charities and the needy (except his own Liberace Foundation for music students), and general hedonism, Lee considered himself a practicing Catholic, and built his palace in the shadow of Palm Springs' foremost Catholic church. Our Lady of Solitude was entirely built with illegal gambling money, according to former mayor Frank Bogert. Today it is a shambles, run-down and locked except during services because the neighborhood is crawling with transients and derelicts. Free sandwiches are handed out from the church rectory door every afternoon. A sign posted there warns people not to knock after the sandwich hour has passed.

▲ Liberace was famously devoted to his mother, Frances, but boyfriend Scott Thorsen found her a battle axe. (Photo courtesy Paul Pospesil Collection)

▲ Friendly, affable Liberace nevertheless kept to himself in Palm Springs. (Photo courtesy Paul Pospesil Collection)

Stefan Hemming, new owner of the Cloisters, opened the house to a gay fundraising event on October 10, 1990, a $50-a-head cocktail party to support the congressional campaign of Democrat Ralph Waite, the former television actor, who was more sympathetic to the AIDS issue than his Republican opponent. The party was officially produced by the Desert Business Association, the Palm Springs gay chamber of commerce.

Liberace would have loved it.

▶ Liberace's tastes ran from French boys to Greek video action. (Photos courtesy Paul Pospesil Collection)

Sally's Balls

$\int$ ALLY EHRENS LIKES TO call herself the "first lady builder in Palm Springs." She and her late husband Sigmund built their magnificent home in the Cahuilla Hills off South Palm Canyon Drive, as well as the first modern air-conditioned hotel in town (the former Crest View at 950 North Indian Avenue), the first contemporary apartment complex (the Riverside Manor), and many private homes.

The Ehrenses constructed their Cahuilla Hills manor thirty-seven years ago, but the style is still strikingly modern. Fine art, Spanish marble, lovely gardens and swimming pools, and dazzling mountain views overwhelm the senses. The vast sunken living room (thirty-seven by thirty-nine feet) with discreet wet bar has entertained legions of guests, including a big crowd for the Lily Pons memorial services last year.

Sig and Sally moved to Palm Springs from Beverly Hills in the early 1950s. Sig was trained as a pharmacist but worked as a builder and was involved in many local civic causes, including the chairmanship of the traffic and parking commission in Palm Springs, the campaign to raise bonds for the airport, and the Chamber of Commerce.

◄ Sig and Sally Ehrens (left) enjoy a cocktail in Palm Springs. They built the first hot tub in town. (Photo courtesy Paul Pospesil Collection)

Their Crest View hotel instituted many amenities which are now common in Palm Springs inns but were unknown in 1956. It had the first "refrigerated air," first blackout drapes, and first complimentary breakfast, and it was the first hotel in town to boast a refrigerator in every room.

Even more impressive, however, was Sally's invention of the first hot therapy pool in a hotel in the United States, with water heated to 105 degrees and pressure jets. It was shaped like a club and pictured in *Cosmopolitan* magazine's May 1959 cover story. Soon, world rank celebrities like oceanographer Jacques Cousteau and actress Lilian Roth were regularly seen around the hot tub.

Sally Ehrens was an actress herself, as Sally Avidon, in Cleveland. She appeared with Jack Paar on WGAR there. "I sing, dance, and tell stories," she laughed. One of her favorite stories is of the time that Frank Bogert, then manager of El Mirador Hotel, came to visit and she told him she'd greatly appreciate his sending her any overflow business from El Mirador. But when he found out the Ehrenses were charging only $22 a day, he said, "I can't send you any business." El Mirador was charging $45 without air conditioning or hot tub!

Following the great success of Crest View and Riverside Manor (built in 1959), Sig and Sally in 1967 bought the La Fonda Hotel and renovated it, rechristening it the Regent. It had a string of lighted balls over the marquee which city architectural commissioner John Mangione objected to as "too garish." Sally insisted the balls were necessary to make the Regent more visible. "How would you look without them?" she kidded John.

Sally Ehrens today is still the kidder, the storyteller, and the hostess extraordinaire. She reigns over the Cahuilla Hills with the warmth and good humor which made her a favorite of old Palm Springs.

Blue
Suede
Shoes

Elvis Alone

▲ Producer Hal Wallis and his wife Martha attend a Desert Museum opening ceremony. Wallis planned most of Elvis' movie roles in Palm Springs. (Photo courtesy Paul Pospesil Collection)

◄ Nudie, at left, renowned as the rodeo tailor; Elvis Presley wears his infamous gold Nudie Suit. (Photo courtesy Nudie Cohen)

E LVIS PRESLEY KEPT TO HIMSELF in the desert, for the most part, and is more associated with Las Vegas or Graceland in Tennessee than with Palm Springs. But he did maintain a fabulous estate in town, where unbridled parties went on, including one—as legend would have it—that ended when a party girl (read whore) died either from an overdose or accidental drowning, and her body was spirited out of the gated complex and clear to Los Angeles.

No police investigation followed.

Producer Hal Wallis did most of the Presley movies and recalls that Elvis and his manager, Colonel Tom Parker, used to come to the Wallis compound in Rancho Mirage, which faces the home of Frank and Barbara Sinatra, to "talk out" the pictures before final scripting.

Edgar L. McCoubrey, founder and owner of Plaza Motors in Palm Springs, was one of many who saw the King around town. One day Elvis, dressed in his all-black trademark style, including silk shirt, black leather jackets, and wraparound black sunglasses, strolled into the car dealership and demanded a black Cadillac—on the spot.

"We explained that we didn't keep black cars in stock because of the desert climate," McCoubrey said. "He wanted it that day. We could order one for him, but he didn't want to wait."

Presley eventually gave up Palm Springs for Vegas, and his house changed hands a few times, winding up with Ray and Joan Kroc as the new owners.

The pool service man says that during Elvis's time the girls draped around the pool were outstanding and always different. Babes gathered around the King, while Colonel Parker tried to shield him from the press. Drink and drugs were rampant. Only the depths of the water know the identity of the dead girl.

135

Bono Knows

Some Vital Statistics
about Palm Springs

Population (1990)	Permanent	Seasonal
Palm Springs	38,394	73,500
Desert Hot Springs	11,221	14,221
Cathedral City	31,750	37,000
Rancho Mirage	12,300	18,099
Palm Desert	20,659	35,000
Indian Wells	2,720	5,186
La Quinta	11,850	15,405

Annual tourist influx population: 1,750,000

Annual days of sunshine: 328

Average annual rainfall: 7 inches

Daily water consumption: 32.6 million gallons (740 gallons per person)

Swimming pools (Palm Springs only): 8,435

Golf courses: 60

Plastic surgeons: 17

Psychiatrists: 18

◄ The heat actually warps the paint on the sidewalk. (Photo courtesy Paul Pospesil Collection)

Air-conditioning contractors: 85

T-shirt shops: countless

Full service hospitals: 4

Charity benefits for hospitals and programs named Sinatra, Hope, Ford, etc.: weekly in season, $15,000 per ticket, no host bar

Daily newspapers: 1 (*The Desert Sun,* which also owns all the weekly newspapers)

Monthly magazines: 1 (*Palm Springs Life,* since *Desert Scene, Country Club,* and other pretenders went under)

Retired Mafiosi: classified

Hotels named for celebrities: Garbo Inn, Harlow Haven, Gene Autry Hotel

Hotels catering to straights: 219

Hotels catering to gays: 27

Average daily high temperature: January, 72° F; July, 110° F (to 125° F)

Piece
of the
Rock

Hudson in the Desert with Tom and Marc

ROCK HUDSON AND HIS WIFE, Phyllis Gates, were "regulars" at the Racquet Club during their marriage (November 1955 to April 1958). Known for enjoying outdoor sports, they were always breathlessly arriving from waterskiing on the Salton Sea or hiking in the Indian Canyons. The marriage, which Hudson told Armistead Maupin was studio-arranged but told others was sincere, indeed ended when Hudson couldn't give up his passion for boys; and thereafter he spent vast amounts of time in Palm Springs with at least two long-term lovers— Tom Clark, who was given a life estate in a desert home in Bermuda Dunes, and Marc Christian, who sued Hudson's estate, claiming he'd been exposed to AIDS.

Rock told his biographer, Sara Davidson, that he needed sexual stimulation on a daily basis. There were widely published rumors that he had "married" another actor—completely untrue, but Hudson was not very discreet and liked to throw parties exclusively for his boys. Jack Coates was one of Rock's first steady live-in lovers. Mark Miller was his personal secretary, introduced him to the joys of long-term stays in the desert, and even tried to hide him in Palm Springs when he was dying. Tom Clark was Rock's traveling companion and lover for ten years, supplanted by blond Marc Christian in the star's final years. Clark remembers when Rock threw his own fiftieth birthday party for his wildly costumed friends and made a grand entrance dressed only in a diaper, to the strains of "You Must Have Been a Beautiful Baby." Later in the evening, he changed into a T-shirt reading "Rock is a Prick." It was a gift from Tom. Hudson succumbed to AIDS on October 2, 1985, in his sixtieth year.

◄ Rock Hudson came to Palm Springs for liaisons with young men. Long-time friend Mark Miller tried to hide Rock's AIDS condition out in the desert. (Photo courtesy Star File)

"He thought his world was going to come to an abrupt and terrible end when he made that announcement, that he had AIDS," the gay novelist Armistead Maupin remembered. "The biggest shock was the fact that 30,000 people wrote and said, 'We love you just the way you are.' It was the biggest revelation of his life, really." Liberace, Maupin added, "never felt the joy of knowing that people knew and didn't care! The sadness of that is that he was a deeply homophobic man. Rock, for all his secrecy, was not homophobic. He saw nothing wrong with the way he was. And when he realized he was going to die and therefore no longer had a career, he said, 'Fuck it, we'll tell the truth.' "

When Marc Christian entered Rock's life, replacing Tom Clark, Clark moved to the desert permanently and Rock continued to visit Palm Springs, staying at the home of Mark Miller and George Nader.

On April 6, 1985, he went with Miller and Nader to Joshua Tree National Monument in the high desert, an hour's drive north of Palm Springs. In that otherworldly lunar landscape of prickly cacti and massive rocks on desolate plains, he made his last visit to the land of so many liaisons, from the Racquet Club to security-gated Bermuda Dunes Country Club.

Tom Clark stayed behind in Bermuda Dunes and wrote a book about Rock which peculiarly never gets around to admitting that they were lovers. He attempts to deny that Hudson had sex with Marc Christian even though knowing he had AIDS. Christian is portrayed as a vicious hustler, blackmailer, and thief, and has sued Clark and his co-author, Dick Kleiner of *The Desert Sun,* after winning a $5.5 million award against the Hudson estate.

Christian hired celebrity lawyer Marvin Mitchelson to file his complaint that the book describes him as "a criminal, a thief, an unclean person, a blackmailer, a psychotic, an extortionist, a forger, a perjurer, a liar, a whore, an arsonist and a squatter." The former boyfriend is asking for $11 million in general damages and $11 million in punitive damages. "The written statements are libelous on their face because Christian is charged with improper and immoral conduct. They aren't backed up by any facts at all." Mitchelson told the Superior Court of Los Angeles. "The most scurrilous one of all was that Marc knew Hudson had AIDS at the time Hudson learned he had it. It says he might have known it before Hudson knew."

"The book stands for itself," Clark said from the desert. "My publishers aren't worried, and neither am I."

The Hidden Power

Walter Annenberg as Emperor of the Desert

P

RIME MINISTER TOSHIKI KAIFU was photographed in his bathing suit, smiling and looking relaxed, at poolside at Walter and Leonore Annenberg's Sunnylands estate in Rancho Mirage during the March 1990 summit meeting with President George Bush. The picture was taken and distributed worldwide by Agence France Presse, which greatly annoyed Annenberg and the local U. S. media, none of whom had been able to gain admission to the fortress-like compound where security forces exceed those at the White House or any other world leader's home.

So who is Annenberg and how can he attract presidents, shahs, and kings to his little place in the desert, and just what goes on behind those oleander and eucalyptus trees, barbed wire fences, and high walls?

It seems positively typical of Palm Springs money stories that Annenberg's family fortune derived from an offshoot of the gambling industry. His father, Moses Louis Annenberg, was an immigrant from Eastern Europe who rose up from poverty to control the nation's largest wire service of horse racing results. His Nationwide News Service, legal in itself, was used by bookies taking illegal race bets, and he used the profits to found a massive publishing empire that included *The Morning Telegraph*, the *Daily Racing Form*, *True Detective* magazine, and the daily *Philadelphia Inquirer*. By the mid-thirties, the elder Annenberg

◀ Lee Annenberg chats it up with Eugene Ormandy, symphony orchestra conductor who dropped in for a little parlor music. (Photo courtesy Paul Pospesil Collection)

was said to have an income of $6 million a year, making him one of the richest men in the world.

He made the mistake of using his power to attack Franklin D. Roosevelt and the New Deal, and FDR quickly retaliated with an IRS investigation that in 1940 convicted Moses of tax evasion charges of $9.6 million. He was sentenced to three years in prison and ultimately died a month after his release. His son, Walter, born March 13, 1908, stood by his side in that Chicago courtroom and watched his father's fall from grace.

As a young man in the twenties and thirties, Walter had been attracted to Hollywood and the life of riotous pleasure, and he had the perfect vehicle in his father's magazine, *Screen Guide,* to enable him to hang around with movie people and spend lost weekends in Palm Springs, dating starlets and staying up all night gambling at the Dunes or the 139 Club. Former mayor Frank Bogert and Annenberg both dated the same actress, June Travis, in the thirties.

Nonetheless, he grew to be a shrewd businessman and managed to create a vastly powerful media empire from the ruins of his father's demolished career. Founder of *Seventeen* and *TV Guide,* among his Triangle Publications, Walter rose to a formidable wealth that even Moses could not have achieved. And he never lost his taste for the desert lifestyle.

Annenberg began acquiring land in Rancho Mirage in 1962 and completed the first stage of Sunnylands construction in 1966. "People thought he was crazy," Bogert remembers, "but he was one smart son of a bitch." He bought adjoining parcels until he'd accumulated the 208 acres the estate now commands. Still based in Philadelphia in the sixties, Annenberg thought of Sunnylands as merely a vacation home, a getaway to allow his wife Lee the sunny California lifestyle she loved. But it became more important than any western White House.

The house contains 32,000 square feet of living area. The living room alone is 6,400 square feet, and the grounds encompass a square mile. The first guest was former president Dwight Eisenhower, who promptly went out and played the private nine-hole golf course, which is laid out so it can be played as twenty-seven holes. Republican presidents would come to view Sunnylands as a second home. Nixon drafted speeches and taped radio programs there—and hid out there during his humiliating 1974 debacle—and Reagan made it his annual locale for New Year's Eve. George Bush is no stranger to the sprawling complex, although he doesn't enjoy the same intensity of friendship with Annenberg that Ike, Nixon, and Reagan—and even Frank Sinatra—have.

When he first built Sunnylands, Annenberg also bought the only water company in Rancho Mirage, to supply his insatiable lawns, pools, and guest bathrooms. He since divested himself of the water stocks at a huge profit. But if (some say when) the water supply dries up in Rancho Mirage, he won't be able to hoard a reservoir for Sunnylands. With his inexhaustible wealth, he'll have to have it piped or trucked in from elsewhere in California. That tradition goes all the way back to Palm Springs founder "Judge" John Guthrie McCallum, who tried to dig a canal across Indian land to divert the Whitewater River thirteen miles across blazing sands into the new oasis. (And the high desert communities near Palm Springs, including Morongo Valley, Yucca Valley, and Joshua Tree, already have some private homes which are forced to have their water trucked in.)

On December 6, 1968, during the Republican Governors Conference in Palm Springs, three future presidents visited Sunnylands—Richard Nixon, who was President-elect at the time, Gerald Ford, who was then Republican House leader, and Governor Ronald Reagan of California. Conspicuously absent was Vice President elect Spiro Agnew, who had opened the conference with a monumental gaffe, declaring Palm Springs to be "Palm Beach."

Nixon chose the occasion to offer Walter Annenberg the single greatest honor in the publisher's singular life: the ambassadorship to Great Britain. "What impresses me most is his strong character," Nixon was quoted as saying. "His balls—his *cojones*."

Annenberg was well aware that his controversial background, his father's imprisonment and death in disgrace (Moses' last words to his son were "It all amounts to nothing"), his schizophrenic son Roger's suicide at age twenty-two (August 7, 1962), his Jewishness, and his lack of previous political experience all conspired to made him an unlikely choice for Ambassador to the Court of St. James, considered the most prestigious diplomatic appointment the new President would make. He also regretted the loss of time at Sunnylands that the job would cost

▲ Frank Sinatra and Leonore Annenberg. He and Barbara got married at the Annenbergs' little place in Rancho Mirage. (Photo courtesy Paul Pospesil Collection)

him. But he accepted the post, and continued to support Nixon with unwavering loyalty even throughout Watergate and Tricky Dick's political demise. In fact, he offered Nixon unlimited use of Sunnylands during his ordeal, and Dick took him up on it. Annenberg's joint in Rancho Mirage was far more protected from the media than any place in Washington, D.C. Nixon celebrated his sixty-first birthday there on

January 9, 1974, because even his compound in San Clemente was surrounded by reporters, and didn't emerge until January 13.

After Nixon's resignation, the former president continued to hang out at Sunnylands, prompting some people, including members of his own family, to argue that Annenberg was carrying loyalty a bit too far. He was replaced as British ambassador almost immediately after Nixon left office.

Annenberg and Ronald Reagan had been friends since the volatile thirties in Hollywood, when Ron was a liberal Democrat and head of the Screen Actors Guild. By the sixties, however, Reagan had turned conservative, and he and Nancy were (and still are) fixtures at Sunnylands, especially on New Year's Eve. Reagan even took time off from running for the Republican nomination for President in 1976 to attend the lavish wedding of Frank Sinatra and Barbara Marx held at Sunnylands.

The art collection at Sunnylands is worth at least $75 million to $100 million and includes the Steuben glass Asiatic collection and what may be the finest collection of French Impressionists and Postimpressionists in private hands. Among the priceless masterpieces are Van Gogh's portrait of the wife of Roulin, postmaster of Arles, and his *White Roses* and *Olive Trees;* Gauguin's *Mother and Daughter;* Monet's *Irises* and his *Garden;* seven sculptures and bronzes by Jean Arp; Steuben's *Carrousel of the Sea;* Renoir's *Daughters of Catulle Mendes;* and, among the moderns, a portrait of Annenberg by his friend Andrew Wyeth (done in 1978).

Despite repeated vows never to lend out the pictures, Annenberg in 1990 toured a show of fifty-four of the finest Impressionist and Postimpressionist works around the Philadelphia Museum of Art, the National Gallery in Washington, and the Los Angeles County Museum of Art. In 1983, he told Thomas Hoving, then director of the Metropolitan Museum of Art in New York, that he planned eventually to open Sunnylands to the public as a museum where people could enjoy the art. More recently, however, there's been rumors of his donating the works to some existing public space. Sunnylands, it would seem, is unlikely to ever be accessible to ordinary humanity.

◄ Ronny and Nancy wouldn't think of spending New Year's Eve anywhere but at Walter and Leonore's place. (Photo courtesy Paul Pospesil Collection)

Walter sold Triangle Publications to Rupert Murdoch for $3 billion in 1988, and now has nothing more to do than host fabulous parties at Sunnylands and make donations to his favorite causes. The liveried servants, maids, chauffeurs, cooks, and security guards are all under orders to avoid the press and maintain absolute silence about what goes on, under pain of dismissal. The Rolls Royces and Lamborghinis pull up to the gate, the driver announces his human cargo, and if they are expected, the great metal gate swings open while heavily armed guards inside the complex rush forward to double check the occupants of the car.

Sunnylands is truly the kind of place where murder could occur and never be discovered—like the time a young actress allegedly died at Elvis Presley's house and the corpse was smuggled out of town. No local or state police force would dare penetrate Annenberg's fort. Who's going to mess with a guy with $3 billion and a list of friends in the highest places?

Even as liberal a Democrat as Kirk Douglas could be, and was, taken in by the rich exclusivity of Sunnylands. Entering the gates on New Year's Eve, 1986, he was relieved of a box of chocolates he was bringing to the Annenbergs—just in case they should be poisoned, perhaps. He was thrilled to be given a private golf cart and a bucket of never-used brand-new golf balls. And to be told, by the ambassador himself, not to replace his golf divots. Special gardeners were hired to do only that. And he found the party "much looser" than what he'd expected from a bunch of Republican millionaires.

Looser? Well, everybody drank and danced, and nobody had to drive home. One suspects the only drugs in attendance were prescription Valium, antidepressants, and Geritol, however. Douglas caught Ron Reagan with a box of Suponeral—French suppositories to aid sleeping—in his hand. George Burns once used them and complained, "My ass is asleep but the rest of me is awake." Reagan had no apparent trouble sleeping through two terms.

Annenberg gave $50 million to the United Negro College Fund in 1990, causing local Palm Springs charities to cry foul. He has in fact donated to the Eisenhower Medical Center and the College of the Desert among other desert causes, but never to the extent of fifty big ones.

▲ Leonore and Walter Annenberg, feted at a Desert Museum bash. (Photo courtesy Paul Pospesil Collection)

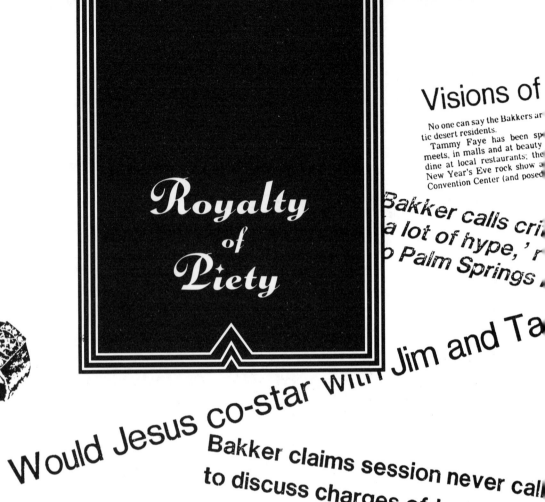

Royalty
of
Piety

Visions of

No one can say the Bakkers ar
tic desert residents.
Tammy Faye has been sp
meets, in malls and at beauty
dine at local restaurants; the
New Year's Eve rock show a
Convention Center (and posed

Bakker calls cri
a lot of hype,'
Palm Springs

Would Jesus co-star with Jim and Ta

Bakker claims session never call
to discuss charges of homosexu

Bakker works as janitor, cleans toilets

Bakker delays plans for new ministr

'We have no cameras, no money,' he says while loading moving

Jim and Tammy Faye Sleaze It Up in P.S.

:sert Holy Land

They've had a chat with local officials about building a $2 billion religious and recreational retreat on 1,700 acres in northeastern Coachella.

No formal application has yet been submitted. A jubilant Coachella mayor has seen only Bakker's hand-sketch of the project. But the

Desert needs flashy people like the Bakkers

Those readers who have moved to the Coachella Valley in the last few months may have wondered why The Desert Sun has placed the latest news of PTL's Jim and Tammy Bakker on our front page.

Is the desert a major fundraising site for PTL?, you may have wondered. Perhaps there's a wellspring of fundamentalism in this corner of Southern California that you haven't yet encountered?

None of the above (as far as we know). It's simply that we feel sort of proprietary about the Bakkers. They're our very own televangelists.

We've housed them, first in the Las Palmas area of Palm

For a while they had a phone call-in setup. You could call, hear a tape, and be asked to "call again tomorrow" to hear more — all for a small fee.

Then Jim came up with a scheme for a giant theme park similar to PTL's Heritage USA, to be situated in Coachella. Officials of that desert town were so spellbound by Bakker's idea they planned much of their budget around it.

Funding for the Coachella project fell through. But that didn't stop Bakker from making a bid, just the other day, to try to buy back PTL. He's an optimist, to say the least. And even now, with a U.S. bankruptcy judge ordering

Faye?

'Praise The Loot': Scandal's just a game to some

ALL OF 1986 AND 1987 found Palm Springs and the nation consumed in the histrionic, hysterical lives of Jim Bakker, the crooked televangelist and builder of the PTL Empire, and his wife, Tammy Faye. Jokes abound about the PTL acronym, but in Palm Springs it was "Pay for Tammy's Lashes." Bob Canon, owner of the Hacienda en Sueno ("House of Dreams"), an intimate hotel on Warm Sands Drive, has a collection of Tammy's eyepieces, which he loves to show to his guests.

The Bakkers moved into Greenbriar Lane in Palm Desert on the first wave of their fortunes, then shifted up to a fancier house with better security in Palm Springs after Jim became embroiled in the Jessica Hahn adultery scandal, amid accusations of homosexuality and embezzlement. Reporters and television crews surrounded the compound at all hours, hoping for a glimpse of the famous religious P. T. Barnum. Palm Springs police guarded the house, protecting the privacy of the town's most famous citizens. Forget Sinatra, Hope, and Dinah Shore—Jim Bakker made the headlines.

Tammy Faye made a game of dressing up in disguise so as to slip past the media, but she could be easily spotted rolling her cart up and down the cosmetics aisle of the local Thrifty Discount store, where spare-change beggars loiter around the doors and housewives in curlers load up on vodka, suntan oils, and cat food at low, low prices.

Jim, for his part, unwisely showed up in some of the most notorious gay-oriented spots in town. "Jim was not only gay, but he was openly so, and known to be gay within the homosexual community in Palm Springs," Canon remembered. He enjoyed the many attractive boys and sizzling social occasions at bars like Shame on the Moon, C. C. Construction Co., Daddy Warbucks, Rocks, Shades, Club III, The Red Raven, and the Club Palm Springs bathhouse. While the baths have been shut down in New York, San Francisco, and other cities as a public health menace, Palm Springs looks the other way.

Events at these spots included whipped-cream wrestling, leather night, fruit Saturdays, short stud contest night (Jim was a natural at 5'6"), boots and shorts party, male bathing beauty night, rusty nail follies, and many female impersonator shows. Tammy could have joined him for the Tammy Why Not show at Daddy's.

Anything but a one-note hedonist, Bakker also slept with women and pissed away other peoples' money. Lots of it, untold millions. Their sixty-five-year-old neighbor, Lilli Marzliker, claimed she made $25,000 in donations to the Bakkers while PTL was still going strong.

When the heat in Palm Springs got too intense, the Bakkers sought treatment (primarily for Tammy Faye's addiction) at the Betty Ford Center, where celebrities can dry out in absolute privacy. After that, Bakker took his son Jamie Charles on trips into the high desert communities of Joshua Tree and Big Bear, ostensibly to go hiking, fishing, or enjoy nature. Instead, he retreated to a cabin and watched TV all day, refusing to call town.

When he was finally defrocked on May 6, 1987, Jim Bakker's leasehold on desert seclusion began to corrode, and by 1988 the infamous couple was forced to sell the Palm Springs house and all its lavish trappings. For a brief time, however, they held the media spotlight on the desert, and, as Canon said, "It's just not half as much fun around here since Jim and Tammy left."

Bakker was convicted of mishandling funds, but his sentence was overturned in 1991 and was under review. The saga goes on.

Father
of the
Groom

NE OF THE FEW legitimate stars who stayed in the desert for good is Kirk Douglas. He and his wife Anne are living national treasures of the shifting sands. Whether throwing out the first ball for the Palm Springs Angels or jumping from one charity ball to the next, they are everywhere.

Spartacus has turned the acting chores over to his son Michael in favor of collecting art in Palm Springs. His home features bronze sculptures, contemporary paintings, pre-Columbian and African pieces everywhere. Anne lived in Paris and worked in a gallery in her early years, where she started collecting works by Chagall, Miró, Utrillo, and others.

Kirk likes primitive art "because I'm fascinated by someone who is not schooled professionally, who has a natural instinct and expresses himself without any academic training."

Yet the Douglas home is unprepossessing compared to grander residences in Rancho Mirage and Palm Desert. The actor has been in town so long he still lives in an older part of the village. And he's humble enough to wait on line for a dinner table at Billy Reed's and gush with unconcealed excitement about an invitation to Walter Annenberg's Sunnylands.

Kirk and Anne have had their share of famous houseguests, of course. Try Robert F. Kennedy and Henry Kissinger for starters. Kennedy left them a bust of himself. Anne recalls when Kirk first took her to Palm Springs in the mid-fifties. "He told us we were going to the Desert," she said. "In the movies, when you hear the word desert, you think of the Sahara. Then you fly over Palm Springs, and you see all those patches of blue and green, which are swimming pools.

"Within two hours of arriving, Kirk and I rented bicycles, and we've never left. For twenty years, I didn't have a single dress in the closet here, only slacks, but now, of course, on Christmas Eve we go to the house of Marvin Davis (owner of Twentieth Century Fox) and they have snow brought in from the studio. So you get dressed up. Yes, the desert changed but not that much. Now I keep one dress.

"Here stars are no longer stars. The differences fade. When Claudette Colbert would come to paint watercolors, and I would go to visit her, I would sit in the room and feel no difference between us. Obviously, I know there is a difference. But the desert is about simplicity."

Kirk told all in his recent autobiography, *The Ragman's Son*. Now he's turned to writing novels, a seemly occupation for a retired desert gentleman. Don't ask him about his famous son. They don't get along that well.

▼ A young "ragman's son," Kirk Douglas found Palm Springs to his liking, and never left. (Photo courtesy Star File)

Sonny Side
of the
Street

IT HAD TO HAPPEN. After all the years that Palm Springs attracted movie stars and celebrities, and after Charlie Farrell was mayor, followed by honorary mayors like Bob and Dolores Hope and Frank Sinatra, it was time for another show business celebrity in City Hall. With Clint Eastwood commanding worldwide media attention as mayor of the tiny coastal resort village of Carmel, the door was thrown open for an entertainer to become mayor of the desert kingdom.

But Sonny Bono? Old-line political insiders didn't give him a prayer of a chance, but the former comedy foil to Cher, out of show business for years, won the 1988 election and proceeded to make greater use of the office for personal publicity than anyone ever dreamed possible. He doesn't have the money, name, or clout of a Hope or a Sinatra, but like them he's taken on the role of a public symbol of Palm Springs.

Born in Detroit to first-generation Sicilian-Americans, Sonny moved to Los Angeles with his family when he was seven and began his professional music career at seventeen, writing "Koko Joe" for Dig Records and the Righteous Brothers. Driving a meat delivery truck on Sunset Boulevard for a living, he dropped his songs off at the record companies and in 1957 started selling them with some regularity to Specialty Records. At that point in his career, Sonny wrote the flip sides of many of Little Richard's hits, but he didn't write the first hit of his

◀ Sonny and Cher in their "I Got You Babe" heyday. (Photo courtesy Michael Ochs Archive)

own until "Needles and Pins," which became a gold record for The Searchers.

Fame arrived in 1964 when Bono and girlfriend Cher Sarkisian recorded "Baby Don't Go" on a borrowed $175. That was followed by "I Got You, Babe," "Bang Bang (My Baby Shot Me Down)," and "The Beat Goes On," all top hits. Within a year, by 1965, Sonny had five songs in the Billboard Top 100, a feat which at the time was matched only by The Beatles. In '66, Sonny and Cher made the movie *Good Times,* an absolutely dreadful piece of garbage which was director William Friedkin's film debut. The picture was screened again at Sonny's first Palm Springs International Film Festival (1990), with both Friedkin and Bono in the sparsely attended theater. Cher had better things to do that day.

Sonny now claims that he and Cher lost popularity because they were the first pop singers to come out against drugs. In any case, they went on the nightclub circuit and had their own television show on CBS from 1971 to 1974, with Cher subjecting Sonny to humiliating put-down jokes. The act and the marriage broke up. Cher went on to far greater fame as a solo. Sonny disappeared into obscurity, doing guest shots on TV and bit parts in films including *Airplane II* and *Escape to Athena.*

Pretty much forgotten by Hollywood by 1982, Sonny went into the restaurant business, opening the first "Bono" restaurant in Tinseltown and following with a second one in Houston. The food is Sicilian-style Italian cuisine based on his mother's recipes. Like Sinatra, Sonny enjoys fooling with pasta sauces. After coming to Palm Springs on vacation for many years, he eventually moved to the desert and sold both restaurants to open his Bono Restaurant and Racquet Club on Indian Avenue, across the street and a few blocks away from the original Racquet Club, which indeed was forced to start calling itself the Original Racquet Club.

Regulars at the restaurant included Elizabeth Taylor (until she got too fat), George Hamilton, Kirk Douglas (one of the few who still lives in Palm Springs), Victoria Principal, and Michael Nader. But with the publicity bonanza his eatery has enjoyed as a result of his mayoralty, the place has gone over to the hoi polloi. Every Yahoo from corny Kansas who visits Palm Springs has to eat or drink at Bono's. You won't find many celebrities there.

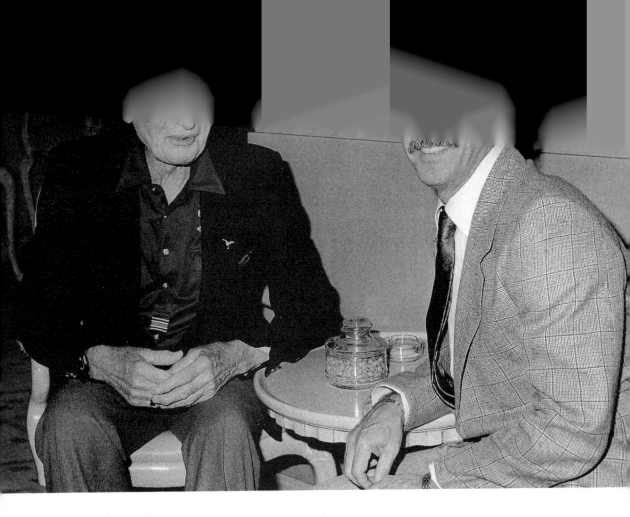

▲ Old-time cowboy star Buddy Ebsen and Palm Springs mayor, U.S. Senate candidate Sonny Bono, in Bono's restaurant where Liz Taylor NEVER eats anymore. (Photo courtesy Paul Pospesil Collection)

As mayor of Palm Springs, Bono's principal focus has seemed to be to use the job to get himself noticed again. And he really succeeds. He grabs headlines, makes appearances on Johnny Carson's "Tonight Show," does a cameo walk-on in a megabucks Bo Jackson shoe commercial, has a line of chocolate chip cookies franchised.

His ideas for improving the town have included a Vintage Grand Prix—loud cars racing down city streets, to the annoyance of the elderly and retired majority—an International Film Festival, and Bicycle-

Mania—all show-business events planned to draw tourists and their money.

But the retail vacancy rate on the main shopping street, Palm Canyon Drive, is about 40 percent, an absolute disaster, and the city's cancellation of its annual payment to the Chamber of Commerce has forced that group to shorten its hours and provide fewer services to visitors. The latest scheme is bringing the Virginia Slims Classic Tennis Tournament to Palm Springs, starting in 1991. They'll play at—you guessed it—Bono Racquet Club.

The one event that is most "successful" in terms of drawing crowds is also the most trouble for Bono. It's Spring Break. Every Easter week, impossible thousands of crazed high school and college students descend on Palm Springs to get riotously drunk, strip and rate girls in the street (on a scale of 1 to 10), jump off hotel balconies, drive around in pickup trucks loaded with shaved ice, beer, and scantily clad youths, break into mob frenzy, smash into palm trees, puke all over the place, and generally wreak mayhem in the normally placid village.

"They just get delirious, and there's nothing we can do," Sonny said in a talk at the Mesquite Country Club, where the gay Desert Business Association had its meet-the-mayor dinner. He promises local residents he will shut down this annual bacchanal, but goes on Johnny Carson to flash pictures of the girls in string bikinis that show almost everything, and makes a great joke of it all. He drives his big ol' Harley Davidson down the strip, personally busting the worst offenders. It's a natural for an AP photo.

Meanwhile, Bonohead ideas for curtailing Spring Break have included banning motorcycles on Palm Canyon Drive during the peak period (a notion favored by the police chief with no apparent concern for any Constitutional rights of bikers); closing down vehicle traffic on the strip altogether (which would just force the Breakers to cruise on smaller, residential streets, citizens howled); and even "smut-busting" the T-shirt shops, demanding that they remove "offensive" language from their windows, crammed with shirts reading "Big Peckers Club," or "Lick It, Slam It, Suck It," or "Jump My Bones." Bono's own T-shirt, "I Want You, Babe," was exempted from the hit list.

In November 1990, the City Council agreed to buy three life-size cardboard cutouts of Bono, so tourists can pose with "Sonny" for a souvenir photo, at a cost projected at $6,000. "It's not my idea," Sonny protested, adding, however, that it was fine with him if the council thought it a good idea.

He's used the city treasury for pet projects like the International Film Festival while Palm Springs swelters in a depressed economy and city deficit. A year after the 1990 festival, Sonny asked the City Council to forgive a $50,000 loan to the festival, and many merchants were persuaded to donate their goods and services in lieu of payment. But Sonny got maximum exposure and publicity from the event.

Finally, it had to happen. Palm Springs is not enough of a platform for the reborn Bono, who launched his campaign for the United States Senate on November 13, 1990, with a press conference at the restaurant attended by a dozen local news people but reported around the world. The restaurant manager borrowed an American flag from a neighbor and planted it in a flower vase, for lack of a flagstand, so that it looked very patriotic hanging behind Sonny on camera, but touched the ground.

Asked why he was running for senator, Sonny told the press, "I dream the impossible dream. I'm that kind of a guy. I follow the yellow brick road."

▲ Sonny Bono, with Buddy Ebsen, at left, officiates as Mayor of Palm Springs, while running for the U.S. Senate on a platform of experience with Cher. (Photo courtesy Paul Pospesil Collection)

▲ Frank Bogert and Sonny Bono. (Photo courtesy Paul Pospesil Collection)

Asked why he considers himself qualified, he said, "Anyone is qualified."

Asked if this wasn't just another publicity stunt, he replied, "With a celebrity like me, people say what does he know about anything? The big factor is name recognition. People recognize my name. . . . I don't feel like I have an expertise for anything. Probably, if I had to fill out a form for the mayor's job, I would never have gotten the job."

If the very idea of Bono in the U. S. Senate seems an impossible dream, or nightmare, just remember Ronnie Reagan. He was once a not-too-talented actor hanging around the Racquet Club. Right now, Bono couldn't get into Sunnylands for a Republican bigwigs' party, but he's rising. He's trying.

Getting a
Break Today

J OAN KROC, WIDOW OF Ray Kroc, the founder of McDonald's and owner of the hapless San Diego Padres baseball team, found more time to spend in her Palm Springs estate, the former Elvis Presley residence, after her husband died in 1984. Ray was a workaholic, driven by ambition or greed to constantly increase his already vast fortunes by selling fatty meats, high-cholesterol greasy potatoes, foamy white bread, and sugary drinks everywhere. ("He's poisoning the world," said Padres pitcher Goose Gossage.) After he died, however, Joan had time to remodel in the desert. She called on Tim Asire, owner of the Palm Desert Paint and Wallpaper store, for Japanese grass wallpapers, string wallpapers, and hand-painted custom purple-fleck foil wallpapers, to redo every room in style. The aesthetic was perhaps garish, but the expense was considerable.

Asire used the leftover pieces of wallpaper to cover the walls of his own house in the high desert town on Morongo Valley, a house that has since become widely known as "the one with Joan Kroc's wallpaper" and was sold on that basis.

I should know. I bought it, and I'm sitting in it right now.

◄ Mr. and Mrs. "Mac" McDonald, founder of the hamburger chain eventually bought out by Ray Kroc. (Photo courtesy Paul Pospesil Collection)

None But the Brave

U. S. Presidents in Palm Springs

E VERY U.S. PRESIDENT since Harry Truman has visited Palm Springs, most of them repeatedly. Harry once made a tremendous scene drinking at the Racquet Club—causing his Secret Service men to try to slip him out the back door, while Truman roared, "I came in the front door and I'm going out the front door!"

But no elected official before or since had the impact that Dwight D. Eisenhower did with his first visit, February 17 to 23, 1954. Television was the new medium in America, and it brought the people lush images of Ike and his wife Mamie on the golf course, basking in the winter sun while the nation shivered. Palm Springs real estate prices boomed overnight. It's fair to say that Ike single-handedly created a desert resort boom.

Mamie's little drinking problem—she was frequently perceived as unstable on her feet, with sloe eyes and slurred voice—started during World War II, when Ike was away on the western front. But she was almost constantly shielded from public appearances in Palm Springs.

The general, as everyone called him, managed to get to Palm Springs as often as possible during his eight years in office and retired here to a winter home from 1962 until his death in 1969. He lived on the fairway of the golf course at Eldorado Country Club in Indian Wells

◄ "You won't see many pictures of Ike and JFK together," said photographer Frank Bogert. (Photo courtesy Frank Bogert Collection)

but got the only hole-in-one of his career on February 6, 1969, at the Seven Lakes Country Club in Palm Springs, six weeks before he died.

Half the monuments in the desert, it seems, are named after him. Eisenhower Medical Center in Rancho Mirage is best known. There's also Eisenhower Mountain in Palm Desert. Eisenhower Drive in Indio, and Eisenhower Rock on the eighteenth fairway at Eldorado.

John F. Kennedy had his famous liaison with Marilyn Monroe in March 1962, and various members of the Kennedy dynasty were frequent visitors to the desert. Lyndon Johnson came in 1964 in a rare joint appearance with Eisenhower to sign a treaty with Mexican president López Mateos, redetermining the Texas-Mexico border.

Richard Nixon took refuge at Annenberg's estate and Nixon's successor, Gerald Ford, liked the desert so much that he's now a permanent resident of Rancho Mirage and has had a major boulevard named after him.

Ford got involved in the 1990 political race for Congress between Al McCandless (R) and former TV Actor Ralph Waite (D) of "The Waltons." Jerry staged a press conference at his home to protest Waite's use of the old desert campaign ploy of asking part-time residents to change their legal voting address to Palm Springs. It's within the law and has been going on in the desert for decades.

(Not that *anyone* believes that votes are accurately counted in the desert. The ballot box is like the census count, eternally debatable. Every Palm Springs mayor since Charlie Farrell has loudly complained that the census doesn't count the actual number of residents. It's hard to do with so many transients, homeless people, illegal aliens afraid of being caught, and a truly squalid shanty town/black ghetto. "The blacks used to have their shacks in Section 14, right in the heart of town, and we were always terrified that *Life* magazine would take a picture. That's why when I came in as mayor, we moved them all out to the north end," said former Mayor Frank Bogert. And there they stay.)

▶ Mamie Eisenhower in 1971. (UPI)

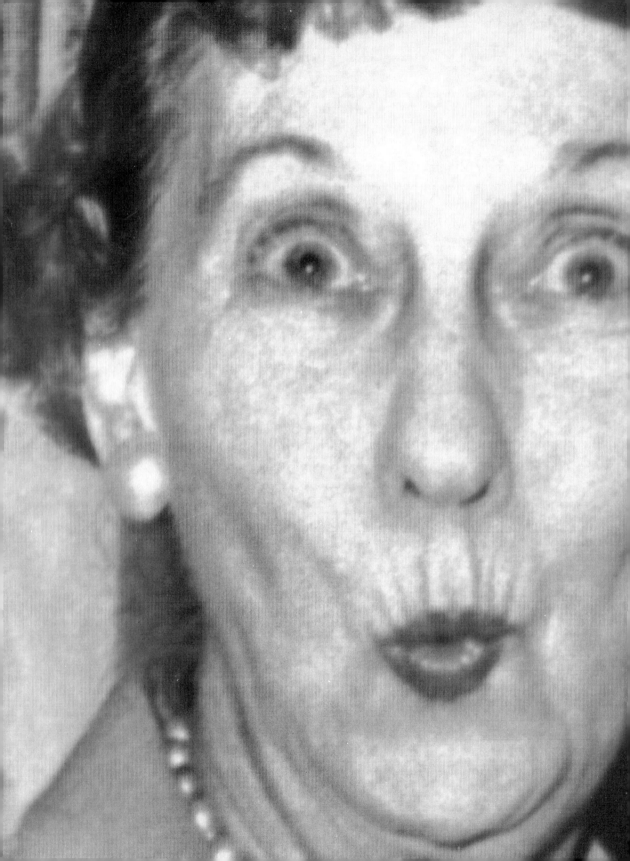

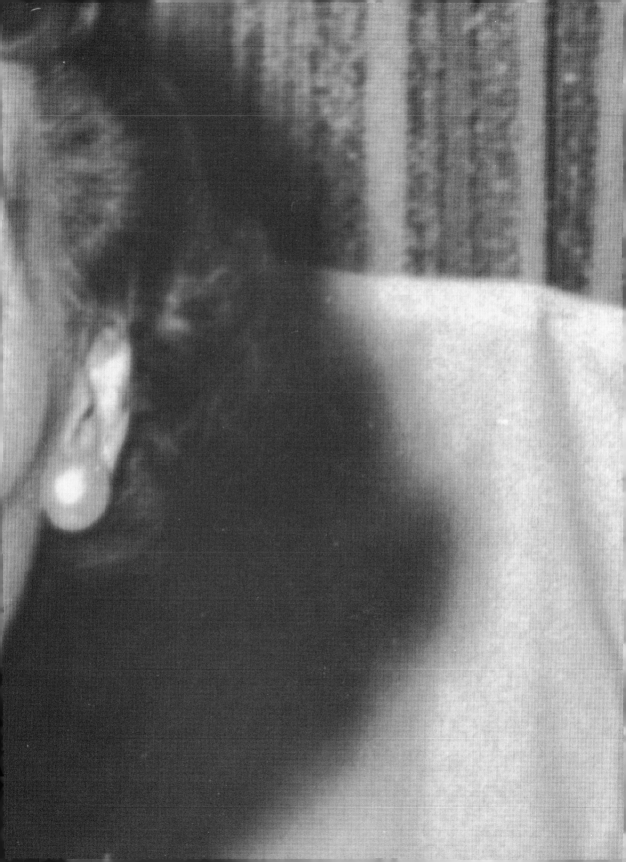

▲ Tricky Dick, Pat, and Ike pose beside a small plane on the open desert landing strip. (Photo courtesy Paul Pospesil Collection)

Jimmy Carter never made more of Palm Springs than a campaign whistle-stop, but Ronald Reagan and George Bush have reinstated the old Republican love affair with the place. Vice President Dan Quayle makes it a regular stop for his golf addiction. Plus, the desert is one of the few places where nobody accuses Quayle of being dumb. Palm Springs doesn't think or make too many intellectual demands on anyone.

▶ Would you buy a used car from this man? (Photo courtesy Star File)

Betty
Bloomer
Ford

Little Lady Takes on the Big Boys

IT CAN'T BE EASY to be Betty Ford, wife of the only former President who was never elected President or even *Vice* President, was widely portrayed as a bumbling idiot, lost the White House to a peanut farmer from Georgia, and now can be seen rummaging through the tomatoes and avocadoes at Ralph's Market in the Smoketree Shopping Center just like any other retiree in shorts.

"I'd like to thank you, Mr. Ford," said a *yenta* buying pineapples. "Since you moved into the neighborhood, my house doubled in value."

But while Gerald was peaking politically, rising far higher than his abilities could carry him, Betty was coping with it by belting down cocktails and following a daily regime of medications prescribed for muscle spasms, arthritis, and sleeplessness—pain pills, tranquilizers, mood alterers. She admits to using all these crutches while living in the White House but claims she was never impaired during official functions. She was widely criticized, however, for narrating "The Nutcracker" with slurred speech during a 1977 broadcast from Moscow.

On April 1, 1978, her family busted her with an "intervention" session and locked her away in the Long Beach Naval Hospital's Alcohol and Drug Rehabilitation Center, where she endured the humiliation of being treated like one of the drunken sailors, even sharing a room with

◄ Betty Ford (right) with Mary Martin (c) and Alice Faye, healing the sick. (Photo courtesy Paul Pospesil Collection)

three other women culprits. But the experience of drying out under harsh circumstances chastened poor Betty. She got up at dawn, made her own bed for the first time in years, and did housekeeping chores. She had meetings and therapy sessions and admitted publicly to being an addict and alcoholic. As she had done earlier with her breast surgery and her facelift, Betty became a public spokesperson for a common medical procedure. In her own way, she was more famous and successful for overcoming adversity than her husband had ever been for backing into the White House.

And she persuaded Eisenhower Medical Center in Rancho Mirage to open the Betty Ford Center, which has got to be the cushiest, most private, most celebrated drug and alcohol rehabilitation center in the world. It's almost *de rigeur* for Hollywood celebrities to check in there, since Elizabeth Taylor made it fashionable, and many of the stars go back and forth, checking in to dry out, then hitting the bottle and pills again when they get out. At $8,000 for a three-week stay, it's cheaper than many luxury hotels and more sequestered from the media.

Dr. Shawn O'Hara, one of the attending physicians at Betty Ford Center, put it this way: "Actors will sometimes play the part of recovering addicts before they are actually recovering." It's a nice way of saying they're lying.

Ricky Nelson went in during his final days as a hard-core addict, when he had to use makeup to venture out in public because he looked so burned out. Nelson died in a 1985 plane crash with his addict fiancée Helen Blair.

Betty Ford herself sometimes leads therapy groups and codependency sessions at the center, according to Sally Manassah, the public relations director for Eisenhower Medical Center, which is far and away the newest, most glamorous and most expensive hospital in the desert. If you must get strung out on drugs and booze, Betty Ford Center is definitely the best place to recover.

◄ Liz Taylor, one of Betty Ford's best customers, during filming of "Malice In Wonderland." (Photo courtesy Star File)

Indian Givers

A Sioux A Sioux

THE AGUA CALIENTE tribe of the Mission band of Cahuilla Indians has been in Palm Springs since before recorded time. Illiterate but cultured, they preserved their history orally in chants and songs, which the elders still teach to the younger members of the tribe.

In 1877, the Southern Pacific railroad was built through Palm Springs to connect Yuma, Arizona, with Los Angeles, and the U.S. federal government rewarded the S.P. with grants of plots of land on alternate sides of the track. The other plots were granted to the Agua Calientes—who must have been somewhat confused at being "given" land they had long considered their own.

Today, the Indians still own half of Palm Springs, most of which is leased out to the white folks until the year 2025. Many homeowners in the city pay a monthly lease fee to the tribe—typically, $50 a month for a house lot. And the famous Spa Hotel on Indian Avenue, site of the orginal sacred hot springs, is on Indian land leased for ninety-nine years in 1957 by developer Sam Banowit. The agreement stipulated that all revenues from the mineral springs would go to the Indians. Banowit also had to move the sacred palm trees at the springs to another location on the property.

Relations between the city and the tribe have never been warm. The Indians resigned their membership in the Palm Springs Chamber of Commerce to protest that the business community in town did not have the tribe's best interests at heart.

▶ Is this the old man of the desert, or what? Palm Springs' Cactus Slim Moorten, progenitor of the Moorten Botanical Gardens. (Photo courtesy Paul Pospesil Collection)

On May 16, 1990, the city announced its "Vision Palm Springs" plan to rebuild the downtown in a sweeping urban renewal. It gave SENCA Real Estate Development Co. the exclusive option to arrange financing and broker the ownership deals needed to tear down and rebuilt most of the mile-square Section 14, containing the Spa Hotel and bordered by Indian, Alejo, Sunrise, and Ramon roads.

The only hitch is that Section 14 is owned by the Indians. But the city never even bothered to inform the tribe of its plans. The Agua Calientes didn't find out about the May 16 action until October, when the information came from the federal Bureau of Indian Affairs, according to Tribal Council chairman Richard Milanovich. And the Indians were plenty mad—mad enough to threaten taking Section 14 back.

"Time and time again, we've seen the city disregard the land use contract we signed in good faith," Milanovich said. "We get promises of open communication. But we don't have it."

Sonny Bono tried to heal the rift with the consolation, "They shouldn't be looking for anything —*devioso*. Nobody's trying to fool them. The Indians need to have a little more faith in Palm Springs." He admitted, however, that the Indians have been cheated again and again in "devioso" dealings of the past.

Starting in 1877, he might have added. But didn't.

◄ Iron Eyes Cody officiates at a Desert Museum gala. (Photo courtesy Paul Pospesil Collection)

Just Hangin' Around

SINGER SARAH VAUGHAN met Frank Sinatra at Pal Joey's restaurant in Palm Springs in the early 1970s. Pat Rizzo, cousin of Frank's right-hand man Jilly Rizzo, was a part owner of the restaurant and brought the two entertainers together. "Before you knew it, she was working for Frank," Pat said.

Vaughan became a regular at Pal Joey's as well as the Chi Chi Club, Ruby's Dunes, and the Cantonese House, all places also frequented by Sinatra.

When she died at sixty-six on April 3, 1990, the flags of Los Angeles flew at half mast, and Palm Springs went into official mourning. Sinatra eulogized:

"She was an instrument and she had an incredible sense of humor. Put those attributes together and we're talking about one of the finest vocalists in the history of pop music."

◄ Sarah Vaughan, the "divine one," met Sinatra at a Palm Springs joint. (Photo courtesy Star File)

The Divine One in the Desert

What's
in a
Name?

A Palm Springs Hoax

THE HARLOW HAVEN in Palm Springs advertises itself with a graphic logo of Jean Harlow and makes claims that it is the former actress's private estate, but evidence indicates otherwise. There was once a family named Harlow who lived there, but they weren't related to the star. "I knew the Harlows real well. They lived here, they went to school here—and they were no relation whatsoever to Jean Harlow," said Frank Bogert. The only Harlow of note was a former mayor of Indio.

The Garbo Inn, a private gay-oriented resort for those who "vant to be alone," makes the assertion that Greta Garbo lived there, but it's not the only hotel in town that claims so. The Ingleside Inn has a card on every table reading, "Garbo slept here."

"Then there's another guy over here who claims that he lives in Will Rogers's house. Well, there was a Rogers family that lived there for twenty years," Bogert added. "I knew 'em. It wasn't Will Rogers. There's a million Rogerses in the world."

And of course there is the notorious Al Capone Cottage at Two Bunch Palms in Desert Hot Springs. "Somebody wants to be a fiction writer," said Billie Lipps, who built the place in 1934. Capone was in Leavenworth and Alcatraz from 1931 to 1939. He was never in Desert Hot Springs to anyone's certain knowledge.

Back in the Saddle

No ONE CAN live in a bottle and build, or maintain, a multi-million dollar enterprise," singing cowboy Gene Autry admitted in his autobiography, commenting on his alcoholism and disastrous failure in the hotel industry.

"My venture into the hotel business was undoubtedly a mistake," he wrote, explaining how he was forced to sell the Ocotillo Lodge in Palm Springs, the Continental in West Hollywood, the Mark Hopkins in San Francisco, and the Sahara Inn in Chicago in order to salvage his remaining inn, the Gene Autry Hotel on Palm Canyon Drive, a desert institution.

The hotel was originally a Holiday Inn built in 1959, made of cinder block and concrete, an ugly and undistinguished "motel" on the outskirts of town, surrounded by sand and tumbling tumbleweeds. (It would have been a motel anywhere but in Palm Springs, where the very word "motel" is prohibited by local statute. Places to sleep have to be called hotel, lodge, inn, or resort.)

Autry bought the tacky property in 1964 as a place to house his new California Angels baseball team franchise when it came to Palm Springs for spring training camp. The team still plays in Palm Springs every March, and stays in the Autry Hotel, but is searching for a way to get out of the obligation. While the other teams have built commodious spring training sites in Arizona and Florida, the Angels are stuck with an outmoded facility in Palm Springs, a tiny ballpark suitable for Class A minor league ball but well below major league standards. The Angels announced in 1990 that they are on a year-to-year basis with

▶ Gene Autry: "No one can live in a bottle . . ." (Photo courtesy Paul Pospesil Collection)

◀ Autry flanked by a girl band at his hotel on South Palm Canyon Drive. (Photo courtesy Paul Pospesil Collection)

Larry Hagman in his J.R. Ewing period with the Singing Cowboy. (Photo courtesy Paul Pospesil Collection)

Angels Stadium (formerly the Polo Grounds, or "Farrell's Folly") and may depart after the 1991 season.

Autry renamed the place Melody Ranch, increased the number of rooms from 107 to 187 and added tennis courts, a second swimming pool, executive suites, and a couple of restaurants and bars. The Sunday Champagne Brunch is an extravaganza of senior citizens getting sloshed over the huge platters of food and flowing bubbly.

In fact, the Autry is a geriatric kind of place these days, not a happening scene. "I couldn't believe we were the only guests under sixty-five in the hotel," said Tia Gindick, forty-four, down from Monterey on a visit.

Autry himself was born in 1907 and a few years ago married a woman much younger than himself, his personal banker from Security Pacific Bank on the main strip of town. Jackie Autry has taken control of his business ventures and is known to the maids and bartenders as a mean, hard-driving, and most of all penny-pinching employer. "Let's put it this way," said a member of the front desk staff, "She wears the pants in the family."

The couple maintain an apartment on the property so she can keep a close eye on the help.

A former food service manager at the Autry remembered livelier days there, when it was new and real stars came by. "One night, I was in charge of the whole staff of waitresses and kitchen help, and we were told that Frank Sinatra was coming by and bringing a dinner group of fifteen to twenty people. So we waited and waited and it got past nine o'clock when the kitchen normally closes, and the cooks wanted to go home. They were tired, the waitresses too. But no, Mr. Autry said we had to wait for Sinatra.

"Well, he finally arrived around eleven-thirty and he was plastered. We had to come up with twenty dinners and drinks for everyone until the bar closed at two in the morning, and even then he didn't want to leave.

"So you know what he left for a tip? Fifteen bucks. That was for the whole staff."

Today the Autry Hotel is mostly booked by the convention trade, which means it's either jam-packed or desolately empty. In the bar, at night, who knows who you might run into—Charlton Heston, Henny Youngman, George Burns maybe.

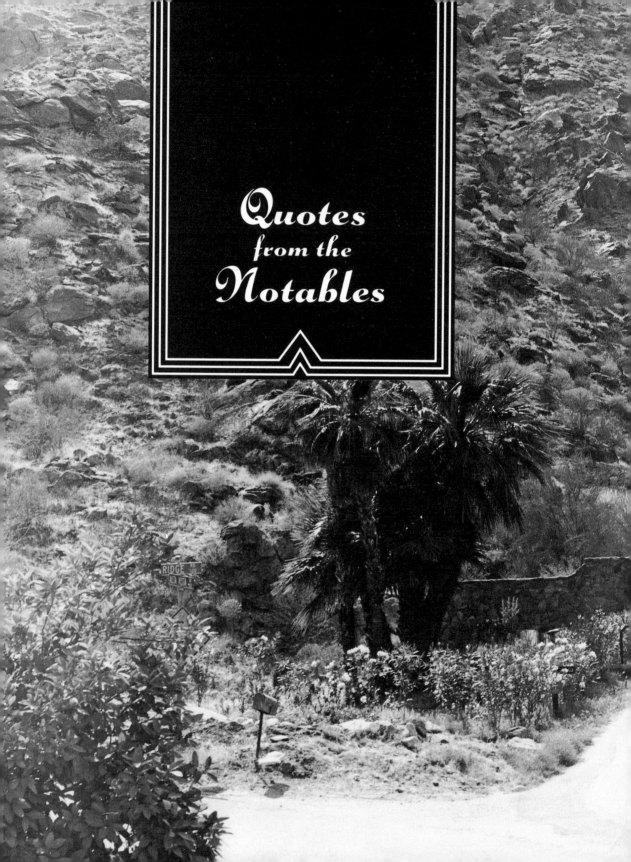

Quotes
from the
Notables

What They've Said About Palm Springs

ROBERT WAGNER: "Palm Springs is like a small town at the turn of the century. There are enough famous people in the desert that it's no longer about being famous. I met the world in the bar at the Racquet Club, meaning I met the Zanucks and the Goldwyns and Cary Grant. I mean, I would see Greta Garbo window shopping. What Palm Springs gave me was a glimpse of belonging."

SHIRLEY JONES: "My blood pressure goes down as soon as I pass San Bernardino. There's a physical release that never fails to surprise me as I'm driving toward the desert."

HAL WALLIS: "It's not the fast lane. But I'll tell you something illogical. Over the years I've maybe gotten more done in the desert—more reading of scripts and books, and more concentrated work—than I have in town. Now, even though I keep an office in town, I find I spend more time here. I play golf three times a week. I'm very active."

VICTORIA PRINCIPAL: "Recovering from something, anything, I always by rote brought myself down here. I've been doing that for fifteen years now. How fancy my lodgings were depended on the state

---

◄ The gated entrance to Suzanne Sommers' desert hideaway estate. Don't even TRY to get through this gate. (Photo courtesy Paul Pospesil Collection)

of my career. But I always know that ten days by myself here will mean I'll review my life, and I'll bounce back. If I get lonely, I call my friends, and they come down." On her first visit to Palm Springs: "Somehow I had come for a party, but I remember knowing literally nobody in California. I wound up going to several parties that night. And I remember being intimidated by the sophistication, the fame."

BOB HOPE: "Go out to Palm Desert. There's so much loot there, they could give Texas food stamps. I don't really sell Palm Springs to people. A couple of years ago at the White House, I remember I started to talk up the desert, and Nancy Reagan looked at me and said, 'Don't! We've already got enough people!' "

JIM LYCETT, former editor, *The Desert Sun:* "If you're a working stiff, you have to have a sense of humor to live here."

JONATHAN SCHWARTZ, New York radio personality: "I was awakened at three in the morning (in the Ocotillo Lodge) by a blaring stereo. . . . The music was recognizable to me as 'Honky Tonk Woman' by the Rolling Stones, an oddly ragged and completely fabulous version I'd never heard. I traced it to a villa on the other side of the pool. The front door was ajar. I pushed it just a bit with my foot. It opened sufficiently to reveal the Stones themselves, Jagger and all, jamming through the night. Women wearing little were everywhere. Empty bottles of Dom Perignon were strewn about like Coors cans. I stayed on till dawn for the best rock session I've ever attended. The Stones, it seems, had given a concert at the Fabulous Forum and had been invited by Dr. Jerry Buss to spend the night at his very own Ocotillo Lodge. It was, he knew, deserted in the heat of June. He hadn't taken into account the one occupied room, his single tenacious customer, a grateful Stones groupie."

A Little Champagne Music

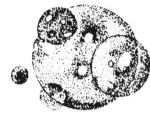

Ah Vun, Ah Two

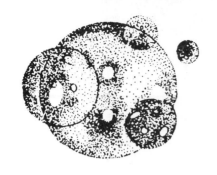

L AWRENCE WELK DOESN'T REALLY live in the desert, but the commercials for his senior citizens' condominium village, Ivey Ranch Country Club, give you the impression that he'll be your next-door neighbor if you buy a $150,000 unit and move in.

Welk, born in 1903, made his money in the "champagne music" soft-core sound favored by the elderly and turned it over in Santa Monica real estate. He built the first high-rise office building there for Union Bank and his own far-flung conglomerate. A religious Catholic, he built his corporate empire on a conservative credo called the Welk Freedom System. The "freedom" he seeks is freedom from government regulation of his business, freedom from unions and their contracts, freedom to fire his people at will.

Long out of show business, he's still selling real estate at Ivey Ranch and elsewhere. The desert complex is located in Thousand Palms, in an otherwise desolate area far from the glamour (and land value) of Palm Springs and the Coachella Valley, on the other side of the sand-blown, Interstate 10 freeway. Other than Welk's walled and low-lying complex, there's not much in Thousand Palms. A couple of gas stations and two burger joints convene at the freeway exit. Shacks are common.

Inside Ivey Ranch, of course, it's better kept. Residents can enjoy their own golf course, swimming, tennis, and other healthy activities in their golden years. One might perish of boredom, however, before seeing the Maestro of Bubbly in person in this godforsaken town. Welk doesn't touch a drop.

203

How Does She Look so Young?

HE'LL KILL YOU if you tell," said Mary Anne Pinkston, Associate Editor of *Palm Springs Life* and editor of the annual Dinah Shore Nabisco golf tournament program, with regard to Dinah's age.

She was seventy-three in 1990, born March 1, 1917, in Winchester, Tennessee, but she thinks people don't know that and won't allow the information included in her P.R. for the tournament, staged since 1972 at Mission Hills Country Club and heavily underwritten by Nabisco.

Dinah never played a stroke of golf in her life before being associated with the tournament, originally sponsored by Colgate. The Shore has become, however, a prestige event for women golfers, and when the March event comes around, Palm Springs is packed with lesbians, who tend to be big fans of women's golf. All the gay women's hotels fill up and the ladies take over the men's hotels for one week only. It happens every spring.

Dinah Denies It

God's
Waiting
Room

The Gay Nineties

FORTY PER CENT of the population of the Coachella Valley (including Indio and Coachella as well as Palm Springs and the other famous towns) is Mexican-American, mostly young families with many kids. John F. Kennedy Hospital in Indio resembles a little Tijuana maternity ward, with record numbers of births every year.

But the world media regards Palm Springs in the light of older celebrities, living and dead. You won't find Madonna or 2 Live Crew or Tom Cruise shopping on Palm Canyon Drive or making their homes in Palm Springs. But you should keep a close eye out for Joey Bishop or Joe DiMaggio. The popular bus tour of stars' homes points out the (mostly former) residences of Mickey Rooney, Doris Day, Cary Grant, Randolph Scott, Howard Hughes (he had seven Palm Springs houses and built a fabulous estate for Marion Davies), Red Skelton, Dinah Shore, Joseph Cotten, Clark Gable, Clifton Webb, Jackie Cooper, and Barbara Stanwyck, who married Robert Taylor, and on and on.

You might hear stories about how world champion figure skater Sonja Henie showed up at the Ranch Club's 1951 circus with a man other than her husband; the celebrated 1955 visit of Pinkie Lee; the time they filmed "Painted Desert"; the years that Eddie Fisher and Debbie Reynolds were together, married and settled in at the Canyon Country Club; when Gloria Swanson lived in Palm Desert and rehearsed her

---

◀ The foursome on the right are Patti Page, Ray Ryan, Louella Parsons, and Jimmy McHue. Looks like somebody spiked Louella's drink. (Photo courtesy Paul Pospesil Collection)

role in "Sunset Boulevard"; how Joli Gabor married Count Edmund de Szigethy and escaped Hungary for Palm Canyon Drive; when Ruby Keeler and Al Jolson were an item at El Mirador; why Vic Damone and Diahann Carroll age gracefully in the desert and never leave; when Peter Lorre and Gilbert Roland and their wives demanded dinner served in the pool at the Racquet Club; where Alan Ladd constructed his building, which still houses the Alan Ladd Hardware Store.

Ad infinitum, the old stuff lingers. But for present-day celebrities, try Sonny Bono.

The Wiefels Mortuary, oldest and largest undertakers in town, is one of the hottest social spots in Palm Springs these days. The death rate from AIDS is also one of the highest in the world, on a par with

▲ Red Skelton was a desert rat par excellence. (Photo courtesy Paul Pospesil Collection)

San Francisco and New York per capita. The desert has a fabulous-variety of well-stocked thrift shops, beneficiaries of the worldly chattel left behind by those who come here to die.

In the long run, of course, the desert is doomed. It is death itself as soon as the water runs out, and despite the cool assurances of politicians that there is no danger of that, common sense indicates otherwise.

▼ Walt Disney in a rare moment of hilarity. (Photo courtesy Paul Pospesil Collection)

The earth is warming from the greenhouse effect, and Palm Springs has been wasting water in a monumental way for decades, keeping its pools filled and its golf courses emerald green. But the population is steadily growing as people are driven out of more congested parts of California by the expense, and the desert offers almost unlimited room to expand on cheap land. The water is not unlimited.

The crime rate is growing as Palm Springs deteriorates. Burglary is so common in a town with thousands of part-time seasonal households that over fifty businesses thrive by offering security systems alone. Some of these are so sophisticated they can determine the difference between a break-in, a fire, and an earthquake. Prostitutes line the blocks of north Indian Avenue, in the shadow of the venerable Racquet Club. Police look the other way. Crime and criminals have always been part of the scene.

Nobody really knows what will happen when the lease expires on the Indian-owned land, fully half of Palm Springs. The tribe will surely not get screwed as royally as it did the first time around. Nowadays they have lawyers. They could take their land back and turn it into legal Bingo parlors if they want to.

The one thing that is absolutely sure to happen, someday, is the Big One. Seismologists agree with uncanny precision that the monster earthquake which is inevitably going to hit Southern California (over 7 on the Richter) will be epicentered in the Palm Springs area. The San Andreas fault line runs down from the High Desert right through town and explodes in the city of Coachella, pinpoint of the devastating temblor.

The Palm Springs newspapers and television stations announce this deadly inevitability with frequency, warning folks to stock up on food, water, first aid supplies, and emergency provisions. Baby tremors and little jiggles are routine stuff, every couple of weeks or so. Yet nobody seems alarmed. Nobody is running for the train to Yuma. Nobody cares. Palm Springs is ready for mortality, maybe eager.

Palm
Springs
Phoenix

VISION PALM SPRINGS IS the idealistic title given to a plan without financial backing but with great inspiration for a revitalized Palm Springs. The basic idea is to tear it down one more time and replace it with all new stuff, hotels and golf courses and shopping, a "destination resort" offering entertainment as well as sunshine and relaxation.

The concept is one of recapturing the lost spirit of the place, renewing the mythology of Palm Springs which has now faded badly. Young people don't come to the desert except to wreak havoc and trash the town during Spring Break. Old people retire here because it's never cold and there are never any steps to climb. Every house, nearly every building, is close to the ground, low-lying in the broiling sun.

Movie stars don't frequent Palm Springs anymore. At the first International Film Festival in 1990, Sonny Bono couldn't produce one bona fide current screen actor or actress in person—although many were promised. Celebrity-seekers watching the limos pull up in front of the Plaza Theater went away disappointed. The city spent $750,000 restoring the old theater in time for the film festival, but it went out of business again shortly thereafter, after trying unsuccessfully to draw audiences for classy art films. Movie houses, profitable ones, went to the multiscreen malls.

What the city fathers should recognize is that the old Palm Springs had charm, glamour, and excitement because of its people. The crusty desert pioneers were joined by an element of free-thinking, free-spending American hedonists, con men, show business tycoons, entrepreneurs, crooks, Californians for whom even the tawdry excesses of Hollywood were not enough. These people made a desert empire, a real old roling one-horse town where everybody let their hair down and anything goes, or went.

Those people are gone and not coming back. The future people of Palm Springs are Spanish-speaking, with the Mexican population now growing at a much faster rate than any other group. May they make a rich barrio, full of culture and color, out of what was once a colony.

Vision Palm Springs is the latest round of some developer's scheme to make a quick buck in the desert. Amazingly, it works at times. Palm Springs was really nothing of a place until 1938, when it incorporated with 936 voters; then it soared to unimaginable heights until it started crashing in the 1970s. Now, we're being told, it will rise again.

Well. Bono. Muy bueno. As long as the Agua is Caliente, or Agua at all, under the blistering sun.